Every Child Needs an Angel

Every Child Needs an Angel

Cosmo Lorusso

iUniverse, Inc.
New York   Bloomington

Every Child Needs an Angel

iUniverse books may be ordered through booksellers or by contacting:

iUniverse
1663 Liberty Drive
Bloomington, IN 47403
www.iuniverse.com
1-800-Authors (1-800-288-4677)

ISBN: 978-1-4502-3499-3 (sc)
ISBN: 978-1-4502-3501-3 (dj)
ISBN: 978-1-4502-3500-6 (ebk)

Printed in the United States of America

iUniverse rev. date: 06/15/2010

Chapter One

Nicole was a natural athlete, at home on a basketball court, on the softball diamond, or on the field hockey field. The summer before she began seventh grade, she and two friends competed in a basketball tournament against all-boy teams and won four out of five games, losing only the final game to a trio of extremely athletic boys. The 2001 school year began with Nicole competing on the Northampton Middle School field hockey team. Doug and Linda made as many games as their schedules allowed, which was most of them. So did Linda's father. That was why he was the first to notice the change in Nicole's running stride.

He was standing with Doug and the rest of the parents on the sidelines, enjoying a brilliant fall day in Pennsylvania's Lehigh Valley. All around him, parents and relatives of the girls from Northampton Middle School shouted out words of encouragement to the girls in orange. But Nicole's grandfather began to grow concerned as he watched number 34 move uncomfortably up and down the field. Finally he asked Doug, "What's wrong with Nicole? She's running kind of stiff." Doug hadn't really noticed, but now he began to study her running motion. He was used to his daughter moving fluidly around the field, faking out defenders and aggressively moving to check the opponents' attackers. As he watched now, he saw what his father-in-law meant. His daughter was laboring to move up and down the field with the flow of the game. She was moving awkwardly and gingerly and showed no signs of her usual explosive bursts of speed. "Something's definitely bothering her," Doug agreed.

"She looks stiff, like she's running on eggshells," his father-in-law observed.

"She hasn't complained of anything lately," Doug said. "When she comes out of the game, we'll ask her."

When Nicole came out for a substitute, Doug made his way over to her. "Are you okay?" he asked.

"Yeah," she replied. "Why?"

"You're running funny."

"Well my back hurts a little, but I'm fine, Dad. Don't worry about it."

"Well let's just let the trainer take a look at you."

Doug guided Nicole to the trainer and expressed his concern to him. The trainer checked Nicole. First he looked for a bruise on her back. Then he asked her to twist her upper torso as he checked for a pulled muscle. He didn't see anything to be concerned about, but said that if the pain didn't go away Doug should take Nicole to a doctor for an evaluation.

But Nicole continued to play field hockey every day and so Doug figured whatever she had couldn't be that bad. Some days were worse than others for Nicole. After one practice she told Linda, It really hurts to bend over."

One day Doug asked Nicole to try and touch her toes without bending her knees. She couldn't, but she told him she used to be able to. "Ever since last week when this pain started, my back's been real stiff," Nicole explained. "I have like no flexibility."

The Sheriffs decided to give it a little more time. They all agreed to just leave it for a little bit and see what happens. If the pain got worse, they would go to a doctor. Doug suggested that, in the meantime, maybe Nicole should limit her activities a little bit.

But she met that suggestion a typical teenager's attitude and tone. "I'm finishing field hockey and I'm going out for the basketball team," she told him. Doug knew he couldn't persuade his daughter otherwise.

During the next few weeks, the pain came and went. Sometimes Nicole was fine for days, and then the pain would hit. In early November, the pain came back with more intensity. Nicole also revealed that she was feeling a tingling sensation going up and down her back and into her legs. "It's a weird feeling. It's like spiders are racing up and down my back and into my legs," she told her parents.

A few days later, Linda found a stretching routine she wanted Nicole to try. She encouraged Nicole to perform this series of exercises in the hopes that they would help eliminate the stiffness in her back and legs.

Nicole did the stretches each day at the urging of her mother, but grew frustrated with them after a few weeks when her flexibility didn't improve. "These aren't doing anything," Nicole told her mom sometime in December. Field hockey season had already turned into basketball season and Nicole noticed that she was actually losing flexibility. She would laugh at practice when she stretched with the team because she couldn't get into the same stretching positions her friends could. It didn't bother her too much because on the court, she was still one of the best players on the team.

Nicole didn't complain about the pain to her coach and she didn't miss a practice, but she did feel her game slipping a bit. She wasn't as fast as she had been and was having difficulty keeping herself in a proper defensive posture.

In late December, Linda allowed Nicole to start using Motrin when the pains were at their worst. The Motrin only helped for a little while and then the pain would come back. As the winter wore on, the pain was coming with more frequency and more severity. Before one weekend basketball tournament in Hershey, Nicole was lying on her hotel bed trying to stretch out her back when her friend Kelsey walked in the room. "Are you all right?" Kelsey asked.

"Yeah. I'm just so stiff," Nicole told her. Nicole had to stretch for over thirty minutes in order to be able to play the next game.

As December gave way to January, the pains and stiffness didn't go away. Then in February, the school nurse, doing a routine yearly check-up on the seventh grade girls, noticed that Nicole had scoliosis, a curvature of the spine. The Sheriffs were concerned because Nicole had never been diagnosed with that before. They couldn't help but wonder if the pain had anything to do with this condition. What kept them from being more aggressive in pursuing medical answers was the fact that Nicole continued to play basketball and play it well. How serious could it be if she could still play basketball they thought?

One morning before school, Linda happened to look in Nicole's room to check on her as she was getting ready. She was shocked to see Nicole lying on her back trying to pull on her jeans. They were stuck, just above her ankles. "What are you doing?" Linda asked her daughter.

"I can't bend over," Nicole said in a matter-of- fact manner. "This is the only way I can get them on."

"Is it hurting you again?" Linda asked.

"Really bad this time, Mom."

Linda helped her pull the jeans up and then helped Nicole off the floor. She put her arm around her daughter in an effort to comfort her. "Why don't you stay home today? We'll see if we can't get to the bottom of this."

"I'll just take the Motrin again today, Mom. That seems to take care of the pain. But I've got to go to school. I've got a math test and basketball practice." Linda knew there was no sense arguing with her. Apparently the pain Nicole felt wasn't strong enough to stop her from doing the things she loved or wanted to do.

When Nicole left for school, Linda called Doug at his school. They were both becoming worried about Nicole's condition. "Doug, you should have seen her this morning. She was in so much pain that she couldn't bend over. She had to lie on the floor to put her jeans on!"

"Should we bring her to someone who could diagnose her problem?" Linda asked. She can't keep going on like this. What are we going to do?"

Doug thought and then realized he had an acquaintance that just might be able to help them. "I'm going to call John Graham today. He's one of the best athletic trainers around. We'll let Nicole start working out with him and see what he thinks."

They agreed on that plan. It was the beginning of March. Their daughter had been enduring this pain since October. Enough was enough.

In Doug's capacity as an athletic director, he had come to know John Graham after their paths had crossed on several occasions. Graham was a renowned strength and conditioning specialist who trained professional and Olympic athletes as well as high school sports teams. He was considered a leading expert on how to develop the speed and strength of athletes. Doug called him and explained what Nicole had been going through, and Graham agreed to see her and made arrangements for her to come see him the following week.

Doug introduced Nicole to Graham at the Allentown Sports Medicine Center. Graham began to put Nicole through some workouts in which she did weight training, agility running, and lots of core stabilization exercises. Graham also tested her flexibility and wasn't happy with the results. "Let's give it a little time and see if it improves," he told Doug. Doug had no choice but to agree.

In April, Graham tested her flexibility again. Instead of improving as he thought it might, it had gotten worse. After a workout session in which Nicole was in obvious pain, Doug met Graham in his office. "What do you think, John?" Doug asked.

"I'm concerned, Doug. She should be getting better, but she's not. She's getting worse. There's something obviously causing this. I just don't know what it is."

"So what do you think we should do?"

"I'm not a doctor, but there's something definitely wrong. I want you to see Dr. Norelli upstairs. He's a non-surgical back doctor whom I trust a lot. I'm going to call him and tell him to see Nicole as soon as possible. I'll tell him it's a rush. It usually takes over a month to get an appointment with him, but I'll do my best to get you in sooner." Doug was pleased when Dr. Norelli said that he could squeeze an appointment in for Nicole on Thursday, April 18th, just three days later.

In the meantime, Nicole continued to deal with the excruciating pain each morning. On Wednesday morning, Nicole's pain brought her to tears. "Honey, just stay home today," Doug told her, but he knew his effort to keep her home was futile.

In physical education class at school, Nicole was competing in the Presidential Fitness Test, a battery of timed callisthenic tests and timed runs. "Just write a note allowing me to take my pillow to school to sit on and I'll be all right," she convinced her father. That night she came home and announced that she did 40 push-ups and 40 sit-ups in each of the minute-long Presidential tests. She also had the third fastest time in the 100-yard dash. When Nicole left the room, Doug turned to Linda and asked, "How bad could her problem be if she could still do all those things in gym class?"

"And finish in the top one percent in her grade," Linda added. Nicole's parents were proud of their daughter's athletic accomplishments.

———

On Thursday, Linda and Doug took Nicole to see Dr. Norelli. Once he learned about her history, he began to examine her. When Nicole took off her shirt, Dr. Norelli immediately noticed a bulging lump on Nicole's spine. He moved his hand up and down her spine and over the lump. "She has a para-spinal mass," he said. "We need to have this checked out as soon as possible." Dr. Norelli scheduled Nicole to have an MRI taken that Sunday. He needed to see what was going on inside Nicole and an MRI would provide him with clear, colorful images that were far more detailed than any x-ray could be.

The only unsettling thing in Doug and Linda's minds was that Dr. Norelli wouldn't be able to see Nicole for two weeks. They were thankful he squeezed her in and was doing something to try and help her, but at the same time, they didn't want to wait that long to find out the results. So Doug phoned Dr. Robert

Marcincin, a highly regarded Lehigh Valley neurologist. Doug explained his predicament to Dr. Marcincin over the phone. He also described the bulge that had just appeared in the middle of her back. "In all honesty, doctor, I'm just a concerned and impatient father calling to see if there's any way you could help us out," Doug confessed.

To the Sheriff's delight, Dr. Marcincin was agreeable. "Bring her in along with the MRI on Monday," he said. "I'll take a look at her. Maybe it's just a slipped disc or something along those lines."

On Sunday, Nicole spent about forty minutes listening to her Walkman as she lay on her back inside a tube at the Lehigh Valley Hospital. All the while, the complicated sensors took photographic images of Nicole's internal structure and organs. Not long after she was done, the technician came out from the processing room with two large envelopes in which contained the MRI film sheets. He handed one to Doug. "We're taking them to Dr. Marcincin tomorrow," Doug told the man. The technician had already been informed of this and said, "I know. And I'll be sure I get these to Dr. Norelli." He tapped the envelope under his arm.

When they got home, Nicole went up to her room to go on the computer. Doug was sitting at the kitchen table staring at the envelope. Curiously, he wondered if he'd be able to see something on the film, so he pulled one of the sheets out from the envelope. Then he held it up to the kitchen light so that the penetrating light would allow him to see the images. Linda saw him doing this and stood next to him and looked up at the film as well. For a while, their gazes were held by what they saw on the film. Linda gasped and then they stood silently staring up. Doug couldn't bring his arm down, nor could they take their eyes off the film. Doug didn't know what to make of it. He just knew it didn't look good. *"What the hell is that?"* he kept asking himself. *"What the hell is that?"* It was clear they were looking at Nicole's spine. He knew that. He just didn't know what those big black blotches were that were spreading out as if they had exploded from a dense black core. Doug was thinking to himself that it looked like a paint ball that hit a wall and splattered its blackness everywhere. Linda was reeling from the sick feeling in her stomach. "I don't know how to read these things," she said, her voice trembling. "Who knows what we're looking at? What do you think, Doug?"

"Dr. Marcincin said she probably has a herniated disc or something along that line," Doug offered. "I don't know what to think of these." Doug glanced at Linda who was staring back at him. Her eyes confirmed what he thought. She was lying. He knew that she knew he was lying too. He put the film sheet back into the envelope. He wanted to think it was a herniated disc with blood in it, but he knew that wasn't what it was. They both knew that what they had just seen was ominous and dangerous to their daughter. The Sheriffs were left with a night of uncertainty and anxiousness. "Thank God I made that appointment with Dr. Marcincin," Doug thought to himself as they headed up to bed.

When he left for school the next day, Doug told Nicole he would come to pick her up at her school around 9:30. Then they would go together to see Dr. Marcincin. At school, Doug was able to get some work done early, and then he began teaching a physical education class in the gymnasium. At around 8:50, Diane, Doug's secretary, appeared in the gym and said, "Doug, Dr. Norelli called. He wants you to call him back as soon as possible." Doug rushed back to his office, a knot in his stomach and a prayer in his head. He got Dr. Norelli on the line and identified himself. Earlier that morning when Dr. Norelli viewed Nicole's MRI, he knew he couldn't wait two weeks to give her the diagnosis. He had to call Doug immediately. Once on the line, Dr. Norelli's words shattered Doug's world. "Doug, I don't know how to tell you this," he started, "but Nicole has cancer."

Doug called Linda as soon as he hung up the phone. She was at her office at PPL, the main supplier of electrical power for the Lehigh Valley. "Linda, you need to go pick Nicole up at school," Doug said.

"Why, what's the matter?" she asked.

"I just got a call from Dr. Norelli. It's cancer. You need to get her. I'll meet you home."

There wasn't time to be grief stricken. Doug and Linda's parental instincts took over. They were on auto-pilot and knew that no matter how they felt, there were things that had to get done now and they would find a way do them. Linda went immediately to her boss. "I've got to go and I've got to go now," Linda said, trembling as she spoke.

When Linda told her boss the news, her boss and another supervisor with whom Linda was close, insisted on driving her to get Nicole. Linda went into the front office of the school and had Nicole paged. Nicole looked like every other healthy middle school child as she walked in to the office. "I thought Dad was picking me up," she said.

"We've had a change in plans," Linda said, trying to mask her emotions. In the hallway, Linda noticed that Nicole didn't have her book bag. "I think you need to pack up all of your things," she said.

"Why?" Nicole asked. "I'll be back later."

Linda didn't respond. She just looked at her daughter. She

couldn't think of what to say and wouldn't have been able to get the words out even if she had. But her look was enough. It told Nicole everything she needed to know. She knew then that the doctors had discovered something terrible in those MRI images. Nicole drew close to her mother who was only able to whisper the word "cancer" to her daughter. Nicole, not fully comprehending what was happening inside her body and uncertain about what the future would bring, began to sob uncontrollably. Linda held onto her baby, and somehow, they made their way out of the school and into Linda's boss's car.

When they got home, Doug was there with Linda's dad as well as their pastor. Nicole got out of the car and ran to Doug, who had his arms wide open for his girl. He held her close as he rubbed her back and whispered, "Everything's going to be okay. We're going to take care of this."

Nicole looked up at him and nodded in the affirmative. There was no hint of tears in her eyes. She was done crying. At some point on the ride home, her competitive upbringing began to manifest itself. She began to rationalize that this disease was no different than a fierce field hockey or basketball opponent. In the way that athletes do, she was steeling herself for the upcoming competition. She was preparing for the game of her life. And she had her game face on.

Just as Linda and Doug were discussing where they should bring Nicole, Doug's cell phone rang. It was Dr. Marcincin. Diane had called him for Doug to let the doctor know what was going on. "Doug, where are you?" the doctor asked.

"We're trying to decide what hospital to go to. We haven't left the house," Doug told him. "Did Diane call you?"

"Yes. She informed me of everything that's happening," Dr. Marcincin said. Look Doug, I want to be honest with you. If that were my daughter, I'd take her to Muhlenberg Hospital."

"You would?"

"Yes I would. Doug, Muhlenberg Hospital is a satellite of the Children's Hospital of Philadelphia and they have two of the best pediatric oncologists in the Northeast on staff."

Doug repeated what Dr. Marcincin had told him to Linda.

"Doug, I'll call there right now and get you in immediately. What do you think?"

"What do you think?" Doug asked Linda.

"If he thinks it's best," she said.

"Okay," Doug told the doctor. "Make the arrangements. We're on our way."

The Sheriff family quickly packed some things, got in the car, and started driving to Muhlenberg, which was about a thirty minute ride away. As they drove west through the Pennsylvania hills, a sense of normalcy came upon them. They were subdued now, having gotten through the emotional jolt of the morning's events. They didn't even talk of the disease. Nicole sat in the back and talked about some of the latest school gossip. Doug put on her favorite radio station and she was able to lose herself in the songs. They were a united family, ready to take on whatever was to come their way.

As they were driving, Doug's cell phone rang. It was Dr. Marcincin. He had delivered on his promise. "If you can be there by noon, they'll be waiting for you," he told Doug.

"We'll be there," Doug confirmed.

The staff at Muhlenberg Children's Hospital was warm and caring right from the start. Doug handed over the MRI's to a nurse. The staff had already phoned for any other x-rays Nicole had done over the last six months. Another nurse took Nicole to a room where they would draw blood immediately to determine whether or not Nicole had Leukemia and to have new x-rays taken. Dr. Julie Stern then guided Nicole, Linda, and Doug into a conference room where they all sat around a table. "Let's get one thing straight right off the bat," Dr. Stern began. "When we discuss medical issues about a patient, we discuss them with the whole family. Now, Nicole, you can choose to leave anytime you want to, but no one is ever going to keep any secrets from you. Are we all clear on that?" she asked. The Sheriffs all nodded.

"What you need to understand is that life as you know it will never be the same again. This disease is going to consume a lot of your time, your energy, and your thoughts. And that goes for all of you." The Sheriffs nodded again. Linda and Doug couldn't know to what extent Dr. Stern's words would be true. Things were happening so fast now that nothing seemed real. They heard the words, but couldn't really internalize them.

"Now onto Nicole's medical condition. The blood test we just conducted is negative for Leukemia. The initial MRI's reveal a mass on the spine that's about the size of a softball. They also reveal spots on the ribs, a lung, and the spine. We're going to need you to take Nicole to our hospital in Philadelphia tonight so we can do some more tests and determine the type of cancer she has and how to attack it. That's really all I can tell you right now. Do you have any questions?"

Nicole spoke up. "Can you tell me if it's really bad or not?"

"I really can't yet, honey. We don't know what kind of cancer you have, so I can't tell you if you have an aggressive type or one

Cosmo Lovusso

that doesn't spread as fast. We'll know more after your tests in Philly. Anything else?" There were no more questions. Dr. Stern was up and putting all of the papers into a folder. "They'll be expecting you in Philly tonight around 6:00. I'm sure I'll see you very soon." She put her hand on Nicole's shoulder. "Hang in there, Nicole."

<hr/>

After calling family and close friends, the Sheriffs packed up their car. Their pastor and his wife led the way because they had been to the children's hospital several times and knew exactly how to get there. After enduring the city's rush hour traffic, the two cars made their way to 34th Street amid the cluster of buildings that make up the Children's Hospital of Philadelphia (CHOP). They found two spots in the multilevel parking garage. Then the pastor and his wife escorted the Sheriff family through the doors of this bastion of pediatric care, all of them silently praying that this was where they would find a cure for Nicole's disease.

Once inside, they found themselves in a spacious atrium, which was both colorful and welcoming. A clerk immediately greeted them and attempted to put them at ease. After Doug and Linda registered Nicole, an attendee quickly showed them all to room 34, a room that looked out on a city that was just beginning to light up in the early spring twilight. Doctors and nurses took turns introducing themselves as they came into and out of the room. Some examined Nicole, others took blood, and another wheeled her out to have more x-rays taken. When Nicole came back to the room, she sat between her parents and watched the Atlanta Braves baseball game that was on TV. Nicole noticed that Kevin Millwood, the pitcher for the Braves that night, wore her number 34. "How about that, Dad," she observed. "Everything has my number. The hospital's on 34th Street, I'm in room 34, the pitcher on TV is number 34. Maybe the number 34 is my angel!"

Things settled down around 11:00 at night. It appeared that no more tests would be performed this day. Around midnight, Doug hugged and kissed Nicole goodnight and told her he would be back tomorrow afternoon. He had to arrange some things at school and needed to be home to do it. Linda settled in on a reclining chair where she would spend the night next to Nicole. Because of the day's events and because of her tiredness, everything seemed like a dream. *How could it be real? How could I wake up and start my day like I always do and end the day lying next to my daughter in a hospital room after finding out that afternoon that she has cancer Linda thought. How could that be real?* These questions and thoughts filled her mind as she drifted in and out of sleep.

Doug managed to make it home by 1:00 in the morning. He was surprised to find four people waiting for him in his driveway at this hour. His principal was there, along with his secretary Diane, and two very dear friends from his school, Len and Dennis. They greeted him with open arms. Doug didn't attempt to hide his emotions. Their simple presence there was a great expression of love. They were there to console and support Doug at a time he most needed it. They talked quietly for a while as Doug relayed the events of the day. They noticed his exhaustion and excused themselves so he could rest. Somehow he made it upstairs and fell into his bed. Sleep came upon him instantly.

In the morning, Doug awoke with a shiver. "Holy smokes! What a dream," he said aloud to himself. He reached for his wife Linda. Her place in their bed was empty. He called out to his daughter: "Nicole!" He waited. "Nicole," he said again, but his voice faded when there was no reply. His eyes began to well with tears as he fell back into his pillow. The exhaustion caused by the emotion of the past day had allowed him to sleep deeply without dreams. But now in the daylight, reality was coming back with a vengeance. It wasn't a dream, he realized. It was a nightmare.

Chapter Two

D oug got out of bed and walked into Nicole's room. He forgot why he was going in there. As he stared into the room to try and remember, he noticed a photo album sitting on her desk shelf. He picked it up and began to turn the pages. He was staring at a photo of a toddler in jean overalls, smiling as she hugged Tweety Bird. He looked at the round-faced girl with glasses and a huge smile. She was always smiling, her red lips always dominating her joyous expressions. She had brought so much happiness to them. They wanted more children, but Linda couldn't get pregnant again. But they no longer regretted that. They were thankful that God had granted them the gift of Nicole. He looked at another photo. She was wearing a white jersey with a black number 34 on the upper right chest. Her hair was pulled back into a ponytail. He noticed she wasn't a child anymore. She was a little woman. He couldn't stop the tears from flowing as he wondered about her future. The words of the doctors echoed relentlessly in his mind: *"Life as you know it will never be the same again."* He shook his head to make the words go away and glanced down at his watch. It was 9:00. He couldn't believe it had only been 24 hours ago when this whirlwind began.

Doug now remembered why he was in Nicole's room. He opened up a suitcase and started to pack it with clothes and underwear for Nicole. Then he called Diane at school and gave her instructions to follow for the day. He made a few more phone calls to family members and friends. He picked up the suitcases he had filled for Nicole and Linda. Then he hurried out the door to his truck. It was time to get back to his wife and daughter at the hospital in Philadelphia.

———

When Doug arrived at the CHOP that afternoon, Linda was on the edge of panic. Nicole had been taken for some more procedures and Linda was sitting alone in the room. When Doug entered, she allowed her wall of strength to come down just a little as she cried and hugged her husband. "They've been doing so many things to her. It's out of control," she began. "They've taken blood, they're taking more x-rays and CAT scans. She hasn't been in this room for more than ten minutes at a time."

Doug remained calm. "Linda, that's what we're here for: so they can do all of these tests and figure out exactly what kind of cancer she's got and then decide how to treat it." He paused and thought a bit. "We're getting her the best treatment there is," he said with conviction as he nodded his head up and down. He turned and looked Linda in the eyes. "They have the best doctors here. We're in good hands." They nodded to each other, a tacit agreement that this was the best approach.

Linda was looking out the window onto the Philadelphia streets. "I called my boss and told her I'd have to quit my job," Linda started. "With all these treatments Nicole's going to need and all the care she'll need, I can't go to work. I'm not leaving her alone anywhere, not for one day. I'm not...."

"What did your boss say?" Doug asked.

"She told me not to worry about that right now. I didn't have to make that decision now. She said that should be the least of my worries. She was really nice about it."

"You have some vacation time you can use first. Then we'll see where things are," Doug said. "We have no idea what treatment she's going to need. Let's just play it by ear."

"Just as long as you know I'm staying right by her side throughout whatever's about to come."

Doug nodded again. There was no doubting the truth of that statement.

On Wednesday, Nicole had to go in for a surgical procedure so the doctors could insert a BROVIAC catheter into her. A BROVIAC is a long, hollow and flexible tube which would be inserted into a large vein close to her heart. This could then be used to give Nicole intravenous fluids or medication for the duration of her treatments.

While this procedure was being performed, a nurse came into Nicole's room where Doug and Linda were waiting. The nurse couldn't help but marvel at the flowers and baskets and cards and balloons that filled up the room. "It's like she's got her own gift shop in here," she said. Linda explained how everything was graciously coming from Nicole's friends and teachers and neighbors. She couldn't hide the pride she felt about the outpouring her daughter had received.

"Mr. and Mrs. Sheriff," the nurse started. "The hospital is getting really crowded and we're going to need to place another patient in the room with Nicole. There's a boy.."

Linda cut her off. "You're going to have Nicole have a boy as a roommate?" she asked in disbelief. "You know Nicole is a 13 year old girl who doesn't really need a boy as her roommate right now."

The nurse continued calmly. "His name is Johnny. He's a 4 year old boy who has just been diagnosed with cancer."

Linda looked at her and immediately settled back. "I thought it was going to be a boy her own age. I'm sorry. I didn't mean to be rude. Of course it would all right. I'm sure Nicole wouldn't mind."

When Nicole woke up from the implant surgery, she was in her room. Through her grogginess she realized there was now an occupant in the bed next to hers. As she focused on the face of the little boy who was sniffling and crying, her own eyes widened when she recognized his face. She had sat with him just yesterday at Muhlenberg Hospital when she was waiting for the doctors to see her. "Hey, Johnny," she whispered. He continued to cry. "Hey, Johnny," she said a little louder. "Remember me? I'm Nicole. I sat with you at the hospital yesterday." He quieted down and nodded his head. He did remember Nicole from their brief time together. When the nurse came close to him, he began to wail. Nicole turned to her mother. "Why's he crying?"

"The nurses are trying to get him ready for surgery so he can have a Broviac put in, and he's just scared," Linda explained.

"Ask the nurse if I can help him."

Linda approached the nurse and explained that Nicole actually knew the boy and thought she might be able to help calm him down. The nurse agreed readily.

Nicole was still lying on her back. She was still considered in recovery from surgery. So she asked the nurse to bring Johnny close to her. He cried harder at first when the nurse picked him up, but then calmed down when he was placed next to Nicole's head. "Hi," she started. "You remember me, right?" He nodded. She continued. "I want to show you something." She pulled at the top of her gown and pulled it down from the neck just enough so he could see the incision in her chest and the Broviac protruding out of it. "They need to put one of these in you," she said calmly. "See, I got one. It doesn't hurt at all. It's nothing but a big giant straw that you can eat things through." She reached out and held his hand. She placed his hand near the tube. "It's okay. It's not going to hurt. Let the nurses take you to get one."

The nurse picked up the calm child and said to Linda, "I can't believe she just came out of surgery and helped this little boy like that."

Johnny looked at Nicole as they were wheeling him out the door. "I'll be here when you get back," she promised him. She smiled and closed her eyes to rest.

Thursday was the day of the final tests. The most telling of all the tests would be the biopsy of the tumor. The doctors would use the results to determine the exact type of cancer Nicole had. Doug explained it as he understood things to Nicole. "It seems they have it narrowed down to two types. There's lymphoma and then there's something called Ewing sarcoma. Of the two, I'm told we're rooting for lymphoma."

"Why?" Nicole asked.

"They have a better chance curing lymphoma than they do Ewing sarcoma: a much better chance."

"Well then, let's hope that's what I have."

Doug left the room and Nicole was alone with her pastor. She was minutes away from undergoing a surgery that would determine the severity of her illness and the type of life she would be able to lead. After a few moments of silent reflection, she turned to the pastor and said, "Pastor, would you say a prayer with me."

The Pastor drew in his breath and marveled at the calm and tranquil manner of this young girl. "Yes. Certainly, Nicole. That's a terrific idea." He moved toward her and reached for her hand. She closed her eyes. "Father in heaven," he began, "we look to you today for strength and comfort. We do not question your will, but hope to have the resolve to carry it through. Bless Nicole. Be with her. And guide her through all that is to come. Amen."

She opened her eyes and looked at her pastor. "Amen," she said with conviction. As she was being wheeled away towards surgery, the pastor put his arm around Linda and said, "Linda, you don't have to worry about her. She's in God's hands. And her faith is deep. I've never had a 13 year old ask me to pray with her before. Her faith is deep. She'll be all right." He nodded assuredly.

During the surgery, the doctors extracted a crude shaving of cells from the para-spinal mass. They would scrutinize this sample under the microscope to determine what type of cells this mass was comprised of. Another sample was sent immediately to a lab where doctors would conduct a more extensive screening. The rest of the mass was left inside of Nicole because it was so close to her spine.

"It's still down to one of two cancers," the doctor told Doug and Linda after viewing the cells. "If it's lymphoma, it's very curable. If it's Ewing sarcoma, then you're in for a long, tough road. My feeling right now is that it's lymphoma. But let's wait to be sure. We will meet you tonight in the conference room around 7:00 to discuss the results."

All Doug and Linda could do was nod and pray.

The lab reports came back that evening as promised and Linda and Doug were summoned to a conference room to meet with a group of doctors called the Musculoskeletal Tumor Team. Nicole was allowed to remain at rest in her room. When the Sheriffs entered, the team was already seated around a large conference table. Linda couldn't help feeling their eyes glaring at them. "*These poor people*," she thought they must be thinking. "*These poor people with this sick, sick girl*." Doug viewed them as if they were a jury about to pronounce a sentence on a convicted criminal. He tried to read their faces to determine the type of sentence they were about to hand down. Would it be lymphoma, the lesser of the two evils? Or would it be Ewing sarcoma, a far more menacing threat to Nicole?

When everyone was seated, a female doctor began to offer a detailed explanation of Nicole's situation. "Mr. and Mrs. Sheriff, as you know, since Nicole has been here we have been performing a battery of tests on her to determine exactly what type of cancer she has. We've completed x-rays of the internal tissues, bones, and organs. We've injected her with radioactive tracers and completed bone scans in which we were trying to detect tumor deposits in her skeleton. We've completed multiple MRI's so that we could get the most detailed pictures possible of the tumor and its surrounding structures. We also conducted CAT scans to get both horizontal and vertical images of her bones and lungs. Finally, we've conducted very specific blood tests. All this has completed what we call the staging of the disease to unquestionably determine the type of cancer Nicole has as well as how far along the cancer has progressed." She paused, looked at the papers in front of her and then stared directly into the eyes of the Sheriffs. "To be quite frank, the news is not good for Nicole. She has a very aggressive type of cancer known as Ewing sarcoma. Not only that, but Nicole's cancer is a stage four, the most severe of the stages. The Ewing sarcoma cells have metastasized to several other areas of her body, including her legs, shoulder, ribs and lungs."

As the doctor went on in her methodic manner, Linda felt herself sinking deeper and deeper into a pit. With each description and prediction, she felt physical pain, as if she were being punched in the stomach. She heard the doctor describing Ewing sarcoma, but she was no longer able to comprehend the information.

The doctor continued. "There are no known causes of Ewing sarcoma and it only accounts for 3 percent of all pediatric bone cancers. Trauma or injury is sometimes involved with the site at the time of diagnosis, but that doesn't appear to be the case this time. It's possible that Nicole could have sustained some type of injury in one of her sporting events, but there's no certainty that that's the cause. We simply don't know what causes Ewing sarcoma. What we do know is that in Nicole's cancer cells, there is a rearrangement of the number 11 and number 22 chromosomes. This translocation is indicative of Ewing sarcoma."

She added one more piece of information that was the final blow to Linda's ability to hold herself together. "Currently, her chance of survival is about 30%," the doctor explained.

Doug was numb. As he sat there he felt as if he were watching himself in a movie. *This couldn't be his life. It couldn't be real life. Things like this didn't really happen to people. His little girl had a*

30% chance of survival? What did that mean really? My little girl is
not going to die! No way!

The doctor moved on in her very practiced manner. She
couldn't allow herself to stop long or the emotions of the family
would diminish her ability to deliver the ill-fated information. She
was practiced enough to conceal her own emotional attachment
to this case and continued to convey the prognosis. "Nicole is in
the hands of a team of experts. We have designed an aggressive
and progressive treatment plan which we can only hope will be
as successful as possible."

The social worker of the team gave Linda and Doug time to
digest the news as well as they could at that moment. "Do you
want us to tell Nicole the news or do you want to do it yourself?"
she asked them. Linda looked at her questioningly. Then Linda
looked at Doug. They nodded to each other. "We'll tell her," Doug
said. "Okay," the social worker said, "but we'll come with you.
I want Nicole to know we're all part of her support team." The
Sheriffs were happy to accept the offer.

The doctors finished by telling them that Nicole would be able
to go home the next day and stay home for the weekend. Then
she would have to check into the Lehigh Valley Hospital pediatric
unit on Monday to begin her treatments. The first phase of her
treatments would be three days of an intensive chemotherapy.
When the meeting was concluded, the Sheriffs thanked the group
and then made their way to Nicole's room.

When Doug entered with the team trailing him, Nicole was
able to read his face. She didn't say anything, but she knew the news
wasn't going to be what they had hoped and prayed for. Doug sat
down on the bed and blinked away the tears in his eyes so he could
look at his daughter. She was already welling up with tears and didn't
even try to wipe her face as the tears flowed down her cheeks.

"It's not the news we were hoping for, honey," he said. He broke down as he uttered, "You have Ewing sarcoma." Linda had her arms wrapped around her daughter and they trembled and cried into each other's shoulders. Doug felt a rage inside of him. He didn't say it, but he kept hearing his own angry and bitter voice. *"Why? Why did this have to happen to Nicole? We're good people who have been devoted to God. How did He let this happen? Why would He do this to us? Why? Why? Why?"*

But then a collective calm enveloped the room. No one spoke as they all isolated themselves in their own thoughts and reflections. Nicole's chest heaved and quivered and she sniffled. Finally her crying subsided. She held a pillow tightly to her body and rocked back and forth. Then she looked up at her father and said, "Dad, we're going to make it. We're going to beat this. We're going to beat it together." Doug was intoxicated by her words. Once again, the athlete in her was speaking, pulling the team together as she faced a formidable challenge. He nodded robustly in the affirmative several times. "Yep," Doug agreed and smiled for what felt like the first time in a long while. "Yep," he repeated. "You're right. You're going to make it. We're all going to keep a positive attitude and we're going to make it together." Nicole smiled at her father, the perfect smile dominating her face. Linda held Nicole's hand and smiled at Doug and then looked around the room. The doctors who were there with them were nodding in agreement too.

Chapter Three

In the hospital room, Nicole was with her mother and grandfather. They were preparing to pack up for home. A nurse found some boxes and brought them up to the room so the Sheriffs would be able to lug everything to the car in as few a trips as possible. Doug's sister Jodi was able to entice Doug to let the others do the packing and to walk with her around the hospital. She was worried about her brother. She had talked to him briefly on the phone the night he first called with the abominable news, but she didn't really get a good sense of how he was handling it and how it was all sinking in. As she watched him at the hospital, she realized she still didn't know what was in his head. He was nonstop motion. He listened to the doctors. He was there to comfort his daughter. He recounted what the doctors had told him and Linda to dozens of people, sometimes over the phone and other times to friends and relatives who came to visit. But she knew it was a façade, an outward appearance of strength while his insides were a contained torrent.

So she and her brother walked away from the commotion of the room and found solace in the endless hospital corridors. As they talked about what was going on she tried to read Doug. His eyes betrayed an exhaustion settling over him. His voice contained a simmering sadness. They spoke with a reverent quietness as passed open rooms of other sick children. They smiled and nodded to other sad parents who they came across and to the doctors and nurses who hurried by them.

Somehow they found themselves on the seventh floor of the hospital where the library for parents was located. The doctors had warned both Doug and Linda not to use the Internet to look up information about the disease. They wanted Doug and Linda to remain positive and told them the body of research that was out there on Ewing sarcoma would be too disconcerting to handle at this time. That didn't stop Doug from walking over to the display of cancer books. As he and Jodi conversed, he was glancing haphazardly over the titles. Then he picked up a book with the words Ewing Sarcoma in the title. He opened the book to a random page and began to read. Jodi stepped up on her toes and read over his shoulder:

People whose cancer has not spread and the tumor is found only below the elbow or below the mid-calf have a five year survival rate of 50 to 80 percent. Unfortunately, the news is not that good for people whose cancer has spread and a tumor is found above the elbow. In this group, only around 25 percent will survive five years...

Doug started to shake. His hands held the book as if in a vice grip and his whole body was taut and trembling. Finally he dropped to his knees and began to sob uncontrollably. He shook his head from side to side and then let it drop, his chin deep into his chest. Jodi stood above and behind her brother. She threw her arms around his shoulders and put her face down on top of his head. She swayed with him from side to side and whispered, "It's going to be all right. It's okay. It's going to be all right." Among the rows of research books and medical journals and before the stolen glances of others who were using the room, Jodi let her brother cry until he was exhausted and had no more tears left to shed.

Finally Doug let out a heavy sigh and closed his eyes. Then he opened them and got slowly back up to his feet. He nodded in the affirmative to her and to himself. He was ready now. Jodi placed her arm in his and together they left the library.

It took two cars to haul home all of the flowers, cards, and gifts Nicole received during her five-day stay at CHOP. She was able to rest at home for the weekend, but then she was up early on Monday as she and her parents made their first trek to Lehigh Valley Hospital to begin an intense chemotherapy treatment. She was barely settled into her room when the technicians entered, wearing masks and gloves as they transported the anticancer drugs, being extremely meticulous in their preparation for administering them. If the drug were to touch the skin, it would cause a severe burn. Nicole's chemotherapy was delivered through her BROVIAC, which would allow it to enter directly into the bloodstream and reach all areas of her body. The plan the doctors would follow was for Nicole to receive alternating combinations of drugs every three to four weeks in varying intensities. In this first three-day segment, Nicole would receive a constant dose of drugs for three days straight.

While Nicole was receiving her treatments at Lehigh Valley Hospital, the Sheriffs planned to follow the routine they established during the week in Philadelphia. Doug developed a schedule that allowed him to have quality time with Nicole and still put in enough time at school to carry out his athletic director duties. He would stay with Nicole until about 9:30 each morning and then head to school where he would stay until about 3:30 in the afternoon. He would then get back to the hospital where he would stay until about 10:30 in the evening and then go home to get some chores done there, finish up some school work, and then get five or six hours of sleep. Linda, on the other hand, would do just what she had done in Philadelphia; she would sleep in Nicole's room each night and remain by Nicole's side all day. She was determined to be with her daughter in everything she would encounter.

One of the things the Sheriffs quickly realized was that their friends and co-workers and community members weren't about to let them go through this alone or without help. From the moment they had gotten home that first weekend, the Sheriffs were inundated with good will. They had come home to find prepared meals waiting for them and a promise that they wouldn't have to worry about making meals for a long time. Various groups and individuals with whom the family was associated, groups like the field hockey and basketball booster clubs and people from their schools and neighborhood, told them not to worry about food because they had enough things to worry about. Even when Doug arrived home after 11:00 at night carrying Nicole and Linda's dirty clothes with him, he would find food waiting for him on the table.

The outpouring of love and affection was never more evident than when Doug received a phone call that Monday at his school from Linda's boss. "Hi, Doug, this is Linda Gier of PPL. How is everything going?"

"We're doing okay. Nicole started her chemotherapy today and we're praying it won't be too hard on her."

"How's Linda holding up?"

"Well, she's with Nicole twenty-four hours a day. She wants to be right with Nicole through everything."

"What mother wouldn't want to be?"

There was a pause. Then Linda Gier started again. "Doug, you know Linda only has so many vacation and sick days coming."

"We know. Linda, you know if it comes down to the job or being with Nicole, Linda's going to be with Nicole," Doug stated.

"I know that and so do all of her co-workers. That's why after I explained to the people here what was going on, they stepped forward and decided to donate some of their vacation days to her. Doug, you tell Linda to stay right by Nicole's side and not to worry about her job here. Tell her she has fifty-two weeks of vacation days coming to her courtesy of her co-workers at PPL."

Doug couldn't talk. Tears were rolling down his cheeks and his throat felt like it was closing. "Doug, are you there?" Linda Gier asked.

"I'm here," he finally said. "I'm just overcome by the generosity of people. Linda, I can't believe the kindness of those people. I'm overwhelmed. I can't wait to tell Linda."

"That's not all," Linda continued. "People have also donated money. I have a check here for about $10,000 for Nicole."

The tears started in Doug again. All he could do was shake his head in disbelief. At last he was able to whisper, "God bless you and the people at PPL, Linda. God bless every one of them for their kindness and generosity."

On Tuesday, Doug entered Nicole's room just as the nurse was replacing an empty bag of medication with a new one. Nicole was watching the nurse, studying her technique. "That should be good for another couple of hours," she told Nicole.

"Thanks," Nicole said. The nurse moved to refill Nicole's water pitcher. "Can I ask you a question?" Nicole asked the nurse.

"Sure, Nicole. You can ask anything to anyone of us."

"How come I don't feel it?" The nurse looked inquisitively at Nicole, unsure of exactly what she was asking. Nicole went on. "The medicine. The chemo. I know it's going in to me, but I don't feel its effects. I thought it was supposed to make me sick and all that."

The nurse's face registered understanding. "Those are the side effects of the drugs you are talking about. Different people react in different ways. You might not get sick right away. It might take a few days for it to kick in. Or you may not get sick at all."

"I thought I was going to be throwing up all over this room."

The nurse laughed. "No, honey. It usually takes a little time before you start that."

"Then I should have eaten dessert!" Nicole said in an angry tone. She had watched her grandmother wither away as she was battling cancer because her grandmother refused to eat. She knew Grammy would have been better off had she eaten more. So Nicole vowed that she would continue to eat, even if she had no appetite and even if she was only going to throw it up.

Doug laughed at her and she threw him a typical teenage glare, head tilted down, rolled eyes looking through the bottom of her forehead. Then she laughed too. "Hi, Daddy," she greeted him. Doug kissed his daughter and his wife who was sitting in her seat by Nicole's bedside.

"I've got some great news for you," Doug said to Nicole. Linda could see he was in an upbeat mood.

"What is it?" Nicole asked.

"Mr. Pierzga called me at school and told me the 76ers will have two tickets waiting for us at Wednesday night's game." Nicole's face lit up. She loved watching basketball and the Philadephia 76ers were her favorite NBA team. Mr. Pierzga had been Nicole's sixth grade math teacher, and when she was in his class, they used to talk all the time about how the 76ers were doing. Doug went on. "Mr. Pierzga said he called the front office and explained what was happening to you and how you were such a big Sixers fan and asked them if they could do something for you. Well, Wednesday night, you're going to be the Fan of the Game."

"That's so cool," Nicole yelled. "I love Mr. Pierzga. He was my favorite teacher in sixth grade."

When Doug told the doctor their plans for Wednesday night, the doctor looked concerned. "What's the problem?" Doug asked.

"I'm not sure if we can get her there on time. We've got a certain amount of chemo that still has to get into her," the doctor explained.

Nicole spoke up now. "Listen, Doc. There's no way I'm missing this Sixer's game. I've got to be there. So you do what you've got to do to get this chemo through me. You've got to do something to help me make this game or I'll just go with this bag hanging out of my arm."

"We can push it through faster," the doctor offered. "I just don't know how the increased intensity and speed is going to affect you."

"I don't care how it affects me," Nicole insisted. "Just do it. I'm going to the game and I'm not letting this stop me."

Nicole had also vowed to herself and to her parents that she was going to lead as normal a life as possible. She wasn't going to let the disease dictate what she could and couldn't do. She wasn't going to let it overwhelm her life. Even when she talked with and saw her friends for the first time after learning she had Ewing sarcoma, she didn't allow them to dwell on it. She pushed the subject aside quickly and made it clear that it wasn't going to be something they talked about a lot. There were a lot of other things to talk about, especially boys.

As promised, the doctors pushed the chemo through her more quickly than planned. Nicole and her dad rushed out of the hospital and got on the southbound North East Extension of the Pennsylvania Turnpike and sped towards Philly. Mr. Pierzga met them in front of the arena and introduced them to the usher who was to take care of them for the night. He guided them right to courtside where Nicole and Doug were able to sit on the bench seats as the team warmed up. She was thrilled when two of her favorite players Eric Snow and Acembe Mutombo came up to her to say hello. She stood next to coach Larry Brown during the National Anthem and saw her image on the big screen that hung over mid-court. Right before tip off, the usher led them to their seats for the game, which were just a few rows from the court.

As the game wore on, Nicole began to feel the first effects of the chemotherapy on her body. "Daddy, I'm not feeling too good," she told him. Doug led her out into the hallway where she fought back a queasy stomach. An older gentleman who was an usher saw them and approached them. "Is everything all right?" he asked. Doug explained how Nicole was there even though she had just finished receiving her last batch of chemo only a few hours before tip-off. The usher told them to follow him and he led them to a door and opened it. They were outside now in the open air. Nicole immediately began to feel better. "Anytime you need to come out here the rest of the night, just let me know," he told them. "I'll get you away from all that crowd and noise." Doug and Nicole thanked him for his kindness and then made their way back to their seats.

Nicole was exhausted by the end of the game and quickly fell asleep in the car on the way home. Somehow, she still made it to school on time the next morning.

Nicole followed the prescribed plan and had two weeks off from her chemo and then went back into the hospital for a five-day treatment. The chemo had begun to take its full effect on Nicole. She would get violently ill and vomit until her throat was sore. But the day after she was finished with her treatments, she would come home from the hospital and go right back to school where she was keeping up with her work and joining her friends in all that they did.

After the second treatment, Nicole was scheduled to see Dr. Stern and Dr. Phil Monteleone so they could assess her body's reaction to the treatment and determine what the next phase would be. The doctors read over charts and asked Nicole a series of questions regarding the impact the chemo was having on her body. Dr. Stern then said, "Let me check the tumor on your back."

"It's shrinking already, you know," Nicole told the doctors.

"It doesn't happen that quickly," Dr. Stern flatly told her.

"I'm telling you, mine has gotten smaller," Nicole insisted. "Check it."

Dr. Stern and Dr. Monteleone were silent as they performed a series of measurements. Then they looked at each other quizzically. They didn't know what to make of their data. They only knew Nicole was right; her tumor had indeed gotten smaller.

"I told you so," Nicole teased.

The doctors laughed with her and began to enjoy her taunting and competitiveness. In their offices when they and their medical staffs discussed their patients, they all talked about Nicole's attitude. She had the psychological make-up of past survivors.

Survivors continued to stay upbeat. They accepted the challenge of the fight the disease was bound to give them, but they were determined to come out victorious. They pushed the doctors and inspired them to think beyond boundaries that may have been set regarding the treatment of cancer patients. And that's just how Nicole was.

As promised, the doctors hid nothing from Nicole and were very candid with their thoughts about her condition. Dr. Stern looked Nicole in the eyes and said, "The chemo's going to start having some bigger effects on your body, Nicole. The vomiting is just the tip of the iceberg. You might want to cut your hair really short pretty soon because now is about the time when you'll start to lose it."

"I'm not going to lose my hair," Nicole insisted. Nicole was trying to dictate the terms of the battle.

"Nicole," Dr, Stern cajoled her, "you can't be that sure, so you better be ready for when it happens."

"*If* it happens," Nicole corrected.

Dr. Stern was willing to concede the game of symantics. "*If* it happens," she agreed.

That week, Linda did convince Nicole to go and order a wig, just in case.

〜〜

The night before Mother's Day, the Sheriffs attended a wedding. Nicole had gone to a hairdresser and had her hair done. She loved the way it looked. On Mother's Day, she had plans to go to breakfast with her church youth group and dinner with her mom and dad at their favorite restaurant, Paolo's. She left her hair up when she went to bed so her hair would look the same the next day when she went out.

The whole family was up early on Sunday. Nicole's Sunday school teacher was on her way over to pick Nicole up and give her a ride to breakfast. Linda was getting dressed for church and Doug had just lathered up his face to shave. The shrill scream was jarring. It pierced through Doug. With his heart racing, he dropped his razor into the sink and ran towards Nicole in her bathroom. Linda arrived a second later.

"Daddy! Daddy, look," she balled. She held out her hands to him and revealed the source of her horror. "Look, Daddy," she cried again. He saw that she held clumps of hair in her hands. She had wet her hair in order to restyle it. But when she pulled the comb through, the hair had started to pull away from her scalp. She ran her hands through her hair again and he saw just how easily it was pulling away.

He pulled her close to him. "It's going to be all right, Sweet Pea. You knew it was bound to happen. But it's going to be all right." He ran his own hands through her hair and came out with a fist full, which he held on to tightly. He couldn't hold back his own tears anymore. The tears started to make canals through the lather that was still on his face. He looked over Nicole's head to Linda who was crying as she stood there helplessly watching. He didn't know what to do and was looking to Linda for direction. The house bell rang and Mrs. Sarley, Nicole's Sunday school teacher was waiting at the door. Linda hurried down to her and ushered her inside and explained the situation. Mrs. Sarley's eyes filled up with tears quickly. Nicole came down now with a towel on her head.

"I can't go to breakfast today like this, Mrs. Sarley," Nicole stated.

"That's okay, honey. We'll do it another time."

"I'm sorry."

"You don't have to apologize, Nicole," Mrs. Sarley said. She made her way to the door and pulled it closed behind her.

Nicole looked at her mother. The tears began to fill her eyes again at the thought of what her head would look like without any hair. Would she be able to handle the stares? What would the other kids at school say? Would she be able to look at herself in the mirror? "What am I going to do, Mom?" she moaned.

"Let me call Sue, my hairdresser," Linda finally suggested. "I'll see if she can come to the house and do something to make it look …" Her voice trailed off in an attempt not to say anything that Nicole would find offensive. She looked at the drying hair on Nicole's head. There were spots where the hair was noticeably thinned. Other sections still had her original length. Still other spots were bare to the scalp. She grabbed the phone and dialed.

"Hello, Sue. This is Linda Sheriff. I'm sorry to call you so early. I know it's Sunday and Mother's Day, but..." Her throat suddenly felt like it was closing. It was hard to get the words out. The tremor in her voice revealed her unsteadiness. "Nicole started to lose her hair this morning. It was coming out in clumps and now we need some help so she can go out. Is it possible for you to come over and do something for her? She's so upset."

Sue quickly agreed to come over and was there within the hour. She cropped the hair close in many places and put it up in clips in others. Then she tri-folded a bandana and wrapped it over the middle of Nicole's head so that some hair showed just over her forehead and some showed behind above the neck. When Nicole saw herself in the mirror, she beamed a radiant smile. Doug and Linda were amazed at how stunning she looked. Her eyes were alive now and she laughed with pure joy. Doug wiped back a tear and couldn't help but think that this disease that was ravaging Nicole from within could not undo his daughter's beauty.

Later that day Doug, Linda, and Nicole kept their reservation at Paolo's. When the waitress who served the family on many occasions came up to the table to take their order, she gazed at Nicole and said, "Nicole, your hair looks great! I love that cut."

Nicole grinned and said, "Thanks." She accepted the compliment graciously. Then the family placed their dinner order. When the waitress moved away from the table, Nicole looked dubiously at her parents. "All right," she said. "Who paid her to say that?" It took the whole dinnertime for Doug and Linda to convince Nicole they had not contrived a plan to make the waitress say what she did.

Chapter Four

Nicole admitted she was glad her mother had insisted that they order a wig *just in case*. When Linda called the wig store the next day, the saleswoman informed her Nicole's wig had just come in. Linda drove Nicole to the store immediately to pick it up. The saleswoman handed Nicole the box. She sat down and pulled off the box top. She reached in and pulled out the wig. It matched her hair color perfectly. Nicole felt the hair and combed it with her fingers. Linda watched silently. Nicole looked up at her mom and their eyes locked. Nicole nodded. "It's perfect," she whispered. She wore it to school the rest of the school year.

With school ending and summer arriving, Nicole was completing her third round of chemotherapy, which required another three day stay at the hospital. The Sheriffs were all together in the room watching a Phillies game when Doctor Stern came in. She had taken a special liking to Nicole. She admired Nicole's fire and enjoyed how the young teenager humorously challenged her findings and critiqued her medical prognostications. She was there today to see how Nicole was responding to the latest round of chemo. "Only two more rounds to go," Dr. Stern reminded

Nicole. "Then you're probably going to need surgery to remove what's left of the tumor in your back."

Nicole looked at her skeptically as if she wouldn't need the surgery. Dr. Stern read this look and said, "I've told you that before. Don't look at me like I've never told you that before."

Nicole gave Dr. Stern the full brunt of a pissed off teenager's glare. "Did you bump your head or something?" Nicole asked Dr. Stern.

"No, I didn't bump my head," Dr. Stern said, giving back Nicole a little attitude.

"You must have bumped your head because I remember telling you when you first told me I might need surgery that I won't need surgery. You must have bumped your head and forgotten."

"Nicole, ninety percent of patients need surgery after they're done with chemo," Dr. Stern stated.

"Well ten percent don't. And I plan on being in the ten percent."

Dr. Stern's gaze turned into one of admiration. Why couldn't she be in the ten percent she thought? "Well good for you," she told Nicole. "I hope you're right. We'll test to find out in about three weeks."

"Oh, I'll be right," Nicole insisted. Doug and Linda shook their heads in amazement at their daughter's conviction.

The school administration, in an effort to allow Doug to be with his daughter and still get his work done, directed the school's computer technician to create a way for Doug to have access to his school files and emails from home. Each morning before he headed to the hospital, Doug would answer his emails, complete any necessary reports or orders that had to be done, and check in with his secretary to confirm the day's workload and schedule. The athletic director's job was one that Doug had always coveted and loved once he got it. He enjoyed the interaction with coaches and athletes. He enjoyed developing more interesting physical education and health curriculums. But as the summer was gaining steam Doug had second thoughts about keeping his job. A good athletic director spends countless hours at school overseeing the many athletic events that go on each day. A good athletic director must be meticulous in planning and scheduling events and officials and ordering equipment. All of the sudden, Doug was relying too much on his secretary to make phone calls and complete orders. He knew that the fall would not be easy for his daughter and that he would want to spend as much time with her as possible and that would keep him away from school events. And so as Nicole was completing her third cycle of chemotherapy with Linda by her side, Doug, after having just thrown a load of laundry into the washing machine, sat down at his computer and wrote a letter to his school administrators in which he told them he was resigning from the athletic director's job and requesting that he be placed back in the classroom as a physical education and health teacher.

On his way over to the hospital, he called Linda at the hospital and told her what he had decided. Linda listened silently with Nicole at her side. "That's your call," she told her husband. "That's a decision you have to make for yourself." Linda decided she would not offer her husband her opinion on his decision. It was a decision only he could make. When she hung up the phone she did have to explain to Nicole what her father was planning to do. Unlike her mother, Nicole did have an opinion about her father's plan and would express it as soon as her daddy walked in the door to her room.

As always, Doug showed up with a smile. He was always happy to see his girl each day. "Hey, Sweet Pea! How are you?"

Nicole was silent and was giving him the cold shoulder. Doug looked at Linda for a clue as to what was bugging Nicole. Linda just shrugged her shoulders. "What's the matter?" Doug asked Nicole, but she just stared out the window and wouldn't acknowledge him. He turned to Linda. "What's wrong?" he asked.

"It's between you and her," Linda told him. Then she got up and left the room.

Doug was left staring at the back of Nicole. When she turned her head he could see she was crying. He sat down next to her and wiped away a tear that was making its way down her cheek. She pulled away abruptly.

"I hear you're quitting your AD's job," she finally let out.

"Yes I am. I think it's for the best," Doug offered.

"It's because of me, right?" she asked.

"Nicole, honey. I'm not sure what's ahead and I want to be sure I can be with you."

"But you love that job."

"I love you more and want to be with you."

"I don't want you quitting because of me. You always told me if you love something you don't stop doing it. You don't let anything stop you from doing it. And now you're letting me stop you from doing something that you love. I don't want to be the reason why you quit your job. I don't want you giving up things because of me. Just think how that makes me feel."

She was crying without holding back now. She turned and looked straight into her father's eyes. "If you quit because of me, I'll be so mad at you. I'll never forgive you or myself."

Doug was speechless. Tears were running down his cheeks as

he sat down next to his daughter and pulled her close to him and drew strength from her. "All right," he said. "All right."

When he got to his car, he tore up the letter. Nicole didn't want pity. She expected him to continue doing what he loved to do. He wasn't about to let her down.

In between her fourth and fifth cycles of chemo, Nicole attended a basketball camp. She was too weak and out of shape to work in with the other campers and so she remained on a side basket, practicing by herself all day long. She performed her dribbling drills and her shooting drills. Then she would sit down and rest. After a while she'd be up again, dribbling to her left and then her right, always working to improve her skills. When Doug picked her up at the end of camp one day, the camp's director strolled over to him and said, "I can't believe your daughter. She's amazing! I've never seen a kid work as diligently as she did all day long. You should really be proud of her." Doug told him he was. Nicole flashed her huge grin and said, "Thanks."

That night after dinner, Nicole was sitting in a chair on her deck behind her house. The Sheriff house was located on the high side of a hilly street in Northampton. Less than a mile away at the bottom of the hills in town are the schools and playing fields. As Nicole sat there, the sounds coming off the fields drifted up to her. She heard the pings of the aluminum bats from the softball games that were being played. Along with that came the cheers of the spectators and the chatter of the players. She could here the thumping of basketballs on the playground basketball courts and the whistle of a coach. While it seemed so close, it was really a world away. Last summer, that had been her world. The ebb and flow of basketball games and field hockey games had been the rhythm of her life. And now she could only play alone on the sides of courts away from other kids. She could no longer throw her body around recklessly and run up and down a court endlessly. For the first time she allowed herself to conduct a demonstration of self pity. She began to cry.

When Doug came out to join her on the deck he immediately noticed the tears. "What's wrong, Sweet Pea?" he asked her.

She shook her head from side to side. It was hard to speak. Her throat felt swollen and her breathing was labored. Finally she stated, "It's not fair. There are so many things I want to do and I can't. It's not fair. Do you hear all of those kids playing? I want to be there and can't be any more!" Doug moved towards her and she quickly fell into his embrace. They stood there for a moment locked together, not speaking. As Nicole's breathing became lighter and the heaving of her chest settled down, the father and his daughter stood there together as the sounds from the park on a summer night serenaded them. After a few more minutes, Nicole pulled away and shook her head up and down. She was okay now. It was over and done with. She was ready to fight on.

The Sheriffs were together in Dr. Stern's office awaiting the results of some recent tests and ready to discuss what the next phase of the battle against this disease would entail. Dr. Stern had Nicole's file opened on her desk in front of her and was rereading the lab results. She shook her head and smiled at Nicole. "Well," Dr. Stern started, "I won't ever doubt what you say again. Congratulations. You're in the ten percent who don't need surgery."

Doug and Linda hugged Nicole. Their eyes were all full of happy tears. This was good news. They knew there was still a long war with Ewing sarcoma ahead of them, but it felt good to have won at least this one battle. Hopefully it was a sign of more victories to come. Nicole was immediately vocal. "I told you, Doc. I told you I'd be in that ten percent. I told you I wouldn't need surgery," she declared. Dr. Stern allowed the Sheriffs a little time to enjoy the good news.

"To be honest with you," Dr. Stern explained. "Your body responded really well to the chemotherapy treatments. As we've discussed, the procedure we used in administering it to you was new. We thought the results would be better, but we never anticipated they would be this much better. We've never had this kind of positive response before."

On the front lines in the fight against Ewing sarcoma, Dr. Stern had seen the disease overwhelm patients with its malignant force. But today, she believed she was witnessing a positive medical breakthrough. "I'd like to be able to document what we've done with Nicole and have it published in a medical journal if that's all right with Nicole." She was talking to Doug and Linda but looking at Nicole. Nicole nodded enthusiastically in agreement. Doug and Linda agreed as well.

"Now the other good news," Dr. Stern began again, "is that we had originally planned a whole month of radiation to make sure we destroy any of the cancerous cells the chemotherapy missed. But because of the chemotherapy success, we're going to be able to reduce the radiation treatments to only 17 days." There were more smiles all around the room.

"However," Dr. Stern continued, "before we begin radiation, we need to perform a procedure called stem cell harvesting. What we need to do is collect these stem cells from your blood before you receive the radiation treatment. Then we freeze them for storage. After your radiation treatments are complete, we put them back into you. This process helps to ensure the recovery of your bone marrow functions, and the ability of your body to produce red and white blood cells as well as platelets."

Nicole listened intently to Dr. Stern. She had become a proactive patient, always asking questions about what she was being given and how that was being delivered. It was rare for Doug and Linda to have to ask the doctors or nurses any questions because Nicole's queries were so thorough and complete. After a pause, Dr. Stern went on talking directly to her 13 year old patient as if she were a fourth year pre-med student.

"What we're going to do is have your parents administer a drug called Neupogen to you at home early every morning. This drug is a cytokine which will stimulate the production of immature and mature bone marrow stem cells. Then you'll need to come to the hospital each day so we can evaluate the stem cell increase in your blood. When we're happy with the number, we'll begin to collect the stem cells from your blood with something called an apheresis machine. We'll collect the blood through a catheter that will be inserted into a vein. When the blood is in the machine, the machine will separate the stem cells from the rest of your blood and then return your blood back into your body. Our plans right now are to do four days of collecting for six hours a day."

"How will you know when you have enough stem cells?" Nicole asked.

Dr. Stern smiled at her, admiring the quality of the question. "The stem cells are easily identified because they have what we call a marker on them that we can easily identify. This marker is called a CD34 antigen. Each day we'll measure the CD34 blood stem cell content and then make a determination of how many days we'll need to harvest and the number of stem cells you'll need after you're finished with radiation."

"There's my number again, Daddy."

Dr. Stern looked quizzically at Doug. Doug began to explain. "Nicole's field hockey and basketball numbers are 34. And ever since she's been diagnosed, everywhere we turn there always seems to be something with a 34 in it. Her room number at CHOP was 34. Driving to the hospital that first time we were behind bus 34 and a taxi numbered 34. We even got lost last month when we went to Gettysburg on highway 34."

"I think the number is like my angel," Nicole said. "It's always with me. It's even in my blood." They all laughed.

"What made you pick number 34 in the first place?" Dr. Stern asked.

"When I was younger, I remember watching football on TV with my dad. There was a special on about one of his favorite players, a running back named Walter Payton. Dad said he was the greatest running back ever and was a great role model to follow. He was a great team player and always tried his best. His number was 34. So when I started playing sports and I had to choose a jersey number, I chose 34. And now it's my angel."

Dr. Stern was impressed once again with the way Nicole conducted herself and how confidently and clearly she expressed herself. But now she had to get back to explaining the timing of all of the medical procedures Nicole was soon to be subjected to.

"Okay. So let's make sure we all know exactly when all of these procedures will take place. The first phase will happen next week. That's when you'll need to be injected with the Neupogen early in the morning and get to the hospital later that same morning. We'll plan that for Monday through Thursday. And count on being in the hospital for about six or seven hours. Then after that, you'll need to meet with the radiologist and begin preparation for 17 days of radiation through the month of August. We'll plan to reintroduce your stem cells to your body in October. That's a whole other process which we'll explain in detail in September." She looked at Nicole. "You got it?" she asked.

"I got it," Nicole said.

The Sheriffs thanked Dr. Stern for her time and her methods and left the doctor's office. Soon they were on the road with the air conditioning blasting in the truck, resembling just another Lehigh Valley family dealing with the heat and humidity of a July day.

Beginning the next Monday, Doug and Nicole woke up at 4:00 AM. He then administered the shot of Neupogen. The night before Nicole would receive her first shot she got to see for the first time the length of the needle her dad would be using to inject the drug. "It's a harpoon," Doug teased her. "So don't give me any lip or I'll harpoon you anytime I want."

She screamed. "Mommy, Daddy said he's going to harpoon me."

"That's nice," Linda replied.

That became one of many running jokes in the Sheriff family. Anytime Doug wanted something from Nicole he'd say, "If you don't do it I'll harpoon you." And Nicole would loudly complain to a jokingly unsympathetic mother.

By 6:00 AM on each of those four days, Doug, Linda, and Nicole were on the road to the Children's Hospital of Philadelphia to begin the long day of stem cell harvesting. In the recovery room each day, Nicole was given an ICEE, a drink of crushed ice and cherry syrup. Nicole noticed that the drink helped to relieve some of the pain caused by the sores in her mouth, which were caused by the chemotherapy. She also noticed the drink was easy on her stomach. She told her dad she wished she had had one of those drinks every time she was in the hospital receiving her chemotherapy treatments. "If I ever have to go through chemo again, I'll definitely want to drink a lot of those," she told Doug.

The stem cell harvesting went as planned, and by the fourth day, the technicians had collected enough stem cells to be used for the stem cell transplant in October. Nicole would be free of the harpoons. However, she was scheduled to meet with a radiation oncologist the next day to discuss preparation for her radiation treatments.

The Sheriffs met with a radiation oncologist and a technologist. The oncologist explained that Nicole's team of doctors decided that she would need 17 days of external beam radiation therapy. Nicole would be subjected to high energy beams of radiation which would penetrate her tissues and deliver the radiation doses deep in her body where the cancer resided. During this planning session, which the doctors referred to as the simulation, the doctors used a machine called a CT simulator to determine the radiation treatment fields. The images obtained from the machine would be transferred to a planning system where a virtual 3-dimensional image of Nicole would be created and the radiation oncologist would determine exactly where the radiation would be directed. When the treatment fields were set, a technician explained to Nicole that she had to mark them with what they called tattoos. These tattoos would be the targets for the radiation each time she received the radiation.

"I don't want tattoos all over my body!" Nicole stated. "It's still summer and I wear a bathing suit and go up to the community pool."

The technician tried to put Nicole at ease. "Don't worry,

honey," she said. "The marks don't come off. You can swim and bathe and shower and that won't affect them. And the tattoos are only as big as pin pricks. If anything, they resemble freckles. Somebody would have to be really close to you to even notice that you have them."

Doug raised his one eyebrow high as he looked directly at Nicole. "So if a boy knows you have these tattoos and can tell me where they are, you're in big trouble."

The oncologist and the technologist laughed hysterically. Nicole was flabbergasted. "Daddy," she said. "I can't believe you. You're so embarrassing some times."

When the technologist was finished making the indelible marks on Nicole's body, the Sheriffs were free to go and told to come back in four days to begin the 17 days of radiation treatment. On the way out, Doug reminded Nicole again, "So remember, if a boy knows you have these marks, we have a problem." Nicole rolled her eyes. Linda laughed. But Doug's was thinking about a boy named Ben, whose name had been popping up around the house lately among Nicole and her friends.

Chapter Five

Nicole had met Ben at a party towards the end of seventh grade. Her friend Ashley really liked him, but Ben spent the whole night talking to Nicole. Ashley was furious with her friend. "How could you do this to me?" Ashley questioned Nicole. She was in a jealous rage. "You knew I liked him."

"We just hit it off," Nicole replied. "I wasn't trying to steal him from you."

Two days later, he asked her out. All summer long, Nicole and her friends fell in and out of love with boys. They obsessed over them. They called each other and talked about who liked whom or which boy was the cutest. They discussed boys while instant messaging each other on their computers. When her friends were over her house and her father wasn't home, Nicole would be the first one to say, "Let's call the boys."

Nicole worried much less about what others would say about her appearance. Towards the end of the school year, when she was with her friend Danielle at a desk cubicle in the back of the school library, Nicole suddenly turned to Danielle and asked, "Do you want to see me without my wig?"

"If you want to show me," Danielle told her, uncertain of what would happen next.

Nicole looked around to check that no one else was around. Then she reached up and grabbed a swath of hair and pulled it back. She lifted the wig up and revealed a head of close cropped hair that was thin and brown. Danielle stared at the sight. In the next instant, Nicole slipped the wig back on and into place. Nicole smiled at Danielle, who was staring now at the wig. Danielle finally allowed her eyes to meet Nicole's. She quietly asked Nicole, "Do you ever miss your hair?"

"Yeah, sometimes," Nicole said nonchalantly. "But I also liked picking out my different wigs. I get to wear whichever one I want on any day. And I never have a bad hair day."

As the summer wore on, Nicole would occasionally shock her friends one at a time by revealing her real hair to them. She always asked for permission, like when she turned to her friend Kera when they were in Nicole's room trying on bathing suits and asked, "Do you want to see me without my wig?" Nicole was testing the limits of what she wanted to reveal to her friends about the toll the chemo was taking on her. At the same time, she was having some fun at their expense. But these acts also allowed the girls to feel more comfortable around Nicole as she endured these changes. Eventually the girls became so accustomed to Nicole and her wigs, that they would entertain themselves with them. One night, up in Nicole's room, her friend Felicia French braided the hair of Nicole's friends as well as several of Nicole's wigs.

Still, Ben's asking her out definitely had a positive impact on her self esteem. And her friends were constantly telling her that with or without hair, she was beautiful. They envied her high cheeks and big eyes. They marveled at the captivating grin that was always on Nicole's face. Doug knew his daughter was beautiful and he wasn't going to make it easy on any boys who tried to hang around.

One night, Nicole and her friends Sam and Danielle were hanging out in front of Nicole's house when some boys pulled up on their bikes. Soon, the boys were off their bikes and were intermingled with the girls, acting cool and feeling confident. Then Mr. Sheriff pulled in the driveway and glared at them. He got out of his truck and looked from the girls to the boys. "Were you guys invited here?" he asked the boys.

"No, sir," they answered.

"Good. Then go home."

Doug stood there until the boys got on their bikes and sheepishly waved goodbye to the girls as they pulled away. Once he saw them off, Doug stepped inside the house without saying a word to the girls.

Try as he might, Doug wasn't going to be able to stop the inevitability that his teenage daughter was interested in teenage boys. Once Nicole realized that her dad might not make life around boys real comfortable, she knew that in order to see or talk to boys, she would have to utilize more clandestine methods.

One night, Doug and Linda were on their front porch talking to Nicole's friend Kelsey's parents. Nicole and Kelsey were in the backyard as far away from the grownups as possible. They were getting bored listening in on bits of the adult conversation. Finally Kelsey said, "I've got to go see Darren one more time before we go." Darren was a boy she had a crush on.

Nicole looked at her. "But your parents said you were going to go in a few minutes."

"Darren only lives halfway down the block. I'll bet I can run there and back before they're done with their conversation," Kelsey stated.

Nicole's eyes grew wide with anticipation. "Go for it," she urged her friend.

Kelsey took off running through the backyards, avoiding the adults on the porch. Nicole waited nervously for her friend, hoping Kelsey's parents would not just now decide it was time to go. Kelsey meanwhile, reached Darren's house and saw that his bedroom window was open. Nicole heard Kelsey's mom say, "We've got to get going." Nicole was moving towards the back fence when she heard Kelsey's voice screaming in the distance, "Darren, I love you!" Nicole yelled for Kelsey to hurry back. Then she heard Kelsey's mom calling for her daughter. At last Kelsey appeared in the backyard, ecstatic about the result of her caper but gasping for air from her all out sprint there and back. Kelsey's mom called for her again and the girls hurried to the front. As Kelsey was leaving with her parents, Nicole whispered to her, "I heard you loud and clear. That was a good one." And the girls laughed at Kelsey's victory.

And so in between her hospital stays as she completed her chemotherapy cycles, Nicole easily fell back in to just being one of the girls, a boy crazy, fun loving adolescent whose only worries were how she looked and if Ben still liked her.

When school started, Nicole and her friend Emily volunteered to be aids in the school's front office. One of the benefits of the job was that it gave them freedom to roam the school to look for friends. Inevitably, Nicole would convince Emily to help her find whichever class Ben was in at the time they were helpers. When they would find him, Nicole would scream and breathe in short bursts and say, "Oh my God. He's so cute." Then she and Emily would hurry back to the office.

As they got bolder, they would feign having to deliver something to one of their friends who happened to be in the same class Ben was in. She would wave to her friends Kera or Ashley and then ultimately turn and look to see if Ben was watching her. Then she would hurry out of the room where she and Emily would giggle their way back to the main office.

When September passed into October, the sense of normalcy that the beginning of school had brought to the Sheriff family disappeared with the advent of the next phase of treatment. Doug and Linda didn't know if Nicole would even make it back for any of the remainder of the school year. They knew at the very least, Nicole wouldn't be back until late spring. It was time for the stem cell transplant. They had been forewarned about the intensity of the process and all of its inherent side effects and potential dangers. Nothing made this as lucid as the day Doug and Linda were asked to sign the papers to permit the treatment. They were also asked to sign papers stating that they were aware of the dangers their daughter would be in throughout the harvesting process but that they wanted the doctors to proceed anyway.

Linda recoiled from the harsh reality the contract laid out. The wording basically said that since Nicole would have absolutely no immune system, she could not be exposed to any type of virus or bacteria at all. If bacteria entered her system at all, she would probably die.

Linda shook as she turned to her husband. "Doug, I can't sign these. We're giving up all rights to protect our daughter from harm. I don't know if I can do this, Doug."

Doug turned to his wife. "I don't think we have any other option at this point. We've come this far; we'll get through this too. It's just one more phase."

And so the Sheriffs signed.

Doug had started to train himself to not think about things that were in the future. He immersed himself in what was most immediate. The future? He couldn't control that, didn't want to think about the most ominous of possibilities the future might hold. But he could handle now. He could handle helping Nicole through this phase that was now upon them. Sometime in the spring, Nicole gave her father a blue beaded bracelet which she had made. As he held the bracelet in his hand that day, he began to tell Nicole how they were going to use the gift together. "Each bead," he began, "represents a step leading to your recovery. Each time we get through a phase, we'll take off another bead." Nicole liked the idea.

And so they had removed beads after each of her five chemotherapy cycles throughout the summer were complete. They then removed two more after each stem cell harvesting was complete. There were only a few more beads left and both the father and the daughter knew that if they could remove the next one, the most arduous and critical battle would be behind them.

Nicole said good-bye to her friends and teachers. Then she and her parents made the trek back to CHOP to begin the stem cell transplant.

The first thing the doctor's needed to assess was what condition Nicole's body was in after having gone through the five cycles of chemo and the stem cell harvesting. They gave her another complete physical exam. They drew blood in order to get a complete blood count and examine the blood chemistries. They also screened the blood for viruses, which could be lethal to Nicole during the transplant process. During each assessment, the doctors, nurses, and technicians explained every test they were performing and further explained to Nicole and her parents what Nicole was about to undergo.

For the final test, the doctor told Nicole he needed to have her perform a few pulmonary function tests. He needed to put her on a stationary bicycle and have her breathe into a tube while she peddled for a thirty-minute time span. When Nicole got to the room where she would undergo the tests, there was an older girl already on the bike and in the middle of the same test Nicole was about to attempt. Nicole and Doug took a seat and couldn't help but watch the girl and listen to her conversing with the doctors.

"When is this thing going to be over?" the girl asked. It was obvious she was having trouble peddling the bike and was agitated that the doctor wouldn't allow her to stop. The doctor didn't answer her and so she painfully peddled on. "I'm sweating my ass off here," she said to the doctor. "I don't really want to do this right now," she moaned.

"Just a little more," the doctor told her patiently. "Hang in there."

"That's easy for you to say," she told him. "You're not the one who has to go through this torture."

The girl kept on peddling half-heartedly. Then after a short time, she started again. "Am I done yet? I'm really exhausted."

"You're an athlete," the doctor told her. "You should know about workouts and pain."

"Well my team's workouts are fun," the girl replied. "This sucks."

Nicole had had enough of listening to the girl complain. Under her breath she muttered to herself, "Oh will you please just shut up."

Doug couldn't help but laugh at his daughter's lack of tolerance for this girl's constant whining.

Finally the girl was told she was finished. She was given a towel and escorted to the door where she met her mother. "I can't believe they put me through this," Nicole heard the girl say to the mother as the door shut behind them.

As Nicole was being hooked up to the heart and lung monitors, she couldn't get that girl's annoying voice out of her head. She looked at the nurse who was attaching a pulse reader to Nicole's fingers. "What sport does that girl who was just in here play?" she inquired. "The doctor said she was an athlete."

"The girl that just finished? She's a cheerleader," the nurse replied.

"Ha!" Nicole laughed out mockingly. "It figures." Nicole never could understand the mentality of someone who only wanted to root for sports and not play them. Then the girls who were cheerleaders tried to say that cheering was a sport. Nicole, the athlete, did not have a lot of respect for cheerleaders who thought that way.

Once Nicole's hook ups were all in place, the doctor told her to start peddling. For the next thirty minutes, Nicole watched a video of various bike tours and peddled with determination as if she were actually on them. She was lost in the Alps when the doctor called, "Time's up." Nicole and Doug were escorted out into another room to await the doctor's assessment of the results.

When the doctor came into the room, he looked at the chart and then back at Nicole. Then he turned to Doug and asked, "What's your daughter being treated for?"

"Ewing sarcoma," Doug answered. "She's just been through five rounds of chemo and two stem cell harvests."

The doctor shook his head. "You would never know from these results," he started to explain. "Your daughter is amazing. I've got results here that say she's normal. This is really amazing. Her lung capacity just shouldn't be this good." He turned to Nicole. "You are an amazing girl. The other doctors will be thrilled with the results of your test."

"What did you expect?" Nicole wisecracked. "I'm an athlete."

That night in Nicole's hospital room, the transplant team came to visit the Sheriffs to make certain the family understood the hazards of the process Nicole was about to undergo and to make certain they all wanted to proceed. The doctors wanted the family to know that once the process is started, serious health problems could develop if the treatment is stopped. The doctors had to be sure the Sheriffs were ready to see this treatment through, no matter how bad it was going to get for Nicole. And they pulled no punches in letting Nicole know that the side effects to the treatment would be nothing less than brutal. The Sheriffs let the doctors know they understood, and they unanimously announced that they were ready.

"Good," one doctor said. "We're ready too." Then he added, "Now you know this first phase will probably keep you here about four to six weeks."

Nicole was calculating something in her head. Then she shook it in the negative. "No way, Doc," she let out. "I'm out of here in three. I'm going to be home for my daddy's birthday on October 30th."

"Don't get your hopes up for that, young lady," the doctor said. "You'll probably be here until at least the second week in November."

"You don't know me, doctor," Nicole deadpanned. "When I say I'm out of here in three, I mean it!"

The doctor saw the futileness of his continuing, so he decided to excuse himself so he could go perform some task that had all of the sudden become urgent to complete.

───

The next day, Nicole was placed in a room with special air filters which would keep her room infection free. She would be allowed no visitors outside of her parents. Once she was settled in, the doctors connected a bag of medicine to an intravenous catheter housed in Nicole's arm, and then opened the connecting tubes to allow a high dose chemotherapy to slowly drip into her. This conditioning regimen, known as bone marrow preparation, would destroy any cancer cells left in Nicole's body and make room in her bone marrow for the cells which would soon be transplanted. Unfortunately, it would also make Nicole feel very sick.

It wasn't long before Nicole was vomiting quarts at a time, every 20 to 30 minutes. As the regimen was carried out, Nicole's body began to reveal its response to the constant dose of the potent chemicals. In her mouth, open sores developed and were burned with each new vomiting spell. As the chemo killed the marrow, it left a residue that coursed throughout Nicole's body and emptied out of every avenue of escape. A putty-like mucous oozed out of her mouth, rectum and vagina.

Nicole's refuge was the computer in her room and the work that she brought with her from school to complete. She was constantly on instant messenger, I-M-ing with friends who all wanted to support her and be with her. Sometimes she carried on five different I-M conversations simultaneously. She also used the computer to type out her school assignments. Doug and Linda tried to persuade her to ease off the work, but she would have none of that. "I'm keeping up with my work," she told her parents, "because I'm not repeating eighth grade. I'm going to ninth grade with my friends."

"But, Honey, maybe it's too much," Linda stated.

"I'm fine. I'll be fine," Nicole said. Then she repeated, "I'm going to ninth grade." Linda let it go. She knew that if Nicole had set her mind to making that happen, there was nothing she was going to do to change it.

And so Nicole would work or play on the computer as the chemo was delivered into her. Every once in a while she would yell, "Dad! Bucket." Then Doug would rush to get the bucket that was always close at hand and she would proceed to heave out her insides. No sooner was she done vomiting that she would be back at the computer I-M –ing and working on her school assignments.

When the conditioning treatment was complete, the doctors gave Nicole a few days rest to recover from the constant feeling of nausea. Then the doctors were ready to insert the new and healthy cells she had harvested the summer before into her body. Once they were inserted, the only thing Nicole could do was wait in her specialized room to see if the infused new cells would "take" in her body.

For the next two weeks, the doctors analyzed Nicole's blood count. Initially, she had low red and white blood cell and platelet counts. Fortunately, her recovery was not hindered by a high fever that often affects stem cell transplant patients. However, despite the constant communication with friends and family on the computer, Nicole started to suffer a depression brought on by her constant isolation. She had always enjoyed being with people. All she had to do to have a good time was be in a room with her friends. It wouldn't be long until someone was doing something silly and the rest of the girls would follow. They would crack each other up and end up in a hug or an embrace and inevitably a pile. Sitting in her hospital room, she missed them so much; there was a touch or a closeness the computer just could not duplicate.

As the third week was coming to a close, things began to look up. The blood counts were approaching normal levels and the platelet count was closing in on the required 15,000 mm she would need in order to be released. She was taking medication that totally controlled the nausea, vomiting, and diarrhea. She was able to digest an oral medication and keep it down for 48 hours, another required benchmark. Nicole knew she was close to going home when the nurses started giving her instructions for how she needed to live once she got home. She couldn't suppress her joy when the doctors came in and told she was free to go check out. It was three weeks to the day of her arrival. She would be home just in time for her Daddy's birthday.

Once home, Nicole was still bound by the rules of isolation. Nicole could still not risk coming in contact with too many people because of the possibility of contracting an infection. Whoever came into the house had to immediately wash their hands with antibacterial soap and put on a surgical mask. The Sheriffs limited who could come into the house to themselves, Linda's dad, and a woman named Sue Carlson, who would soon take on the position of Nicole's second mom.

Sue was a guidance counselor at the elementary school Nicole attended. When she and Nicole first met when Nicole was in the sixth grade, they immediately took a liking to each other, even after their relationship had gotten off to an inauspicious start. One day, Nicole sat in Mrs. Carlson's unoccupied office waiting for her to return. For some reason that even an adolescent couldn't explain, Nicole started to rummage through her counselor's desk drawers. When Sue came through her door and saw what Nicole was doing, she immediately reprimanded her and followed that up with a phone call home. For whatever reason, this didn't discourage Nicole from coming back to visit Mrs. Carlson. There was something that attracted Nicole to her counselor and something the counselor liked in the girl.

Before long, when one of her friends was having a bad day, Nicole would take her by the hand and lead her to Sue's office. "I've got another one for you," Nicole would announce to her counselor. Sue began to admire Nicole's passion for making other people feel better. She loved her genuine personality and the way she joked and made others laugh.

When eighth grade began and Sue was made aware of how much school Nicole was going to miss, she phoned the Sheriffs and informed them that she would be Nicole's homebound tutor. She vowed to help Nicole keep up with her school work and make it to ninth grade with her friends. Nicole appreciated what her counselor was doing for her, and she continued to work diligently to have all assignments complete by the time of Sue's next visit. Nicole also looked forward to the sessions because they became a time for her to talk openly about what was happening to her in her life. She didn't have to hold anything back and she didn't have to protect Sue from her reality the way she needed to protect her parents from it.

About a week after Nicole came home, a secretary from the middle school called the Sheriff's house and asked to talk to Linda. "Can you to drive Nicole up to the school later today?" the woman asked Linda.

"I'm sorry, but Nicole is under doctor's orders that she can't be around people," Linda responded. "She won't be able to come in or come close to anybody."

"I know that," the secretary stated. "Just trust me and bring her up around one o'clock. Park in the front of the school, and wait outside by the curb in front of the main doors."

Linda curiously agreed to follow the instructions.

Nicole was just happy to get out of the house. Linda didn't tell her where they were going. She drove around town for a little bit and then as it was approaching one o'clock, headed over towards the middle school. She pulled up in front as she had been instructed to do and parked the car. "What are we doing here?" Nicole asked. Linda truthfully responded, "I don't know, but let's get out for a second."

It was the middle of the school day, yet the school itself was eerily quiet. The mother and daughter got out of the car and stepped onto the wide sidewalk that led to the front doors of the school. Nicole immediately felt a shiver come over her from the coolness of the late October afternoon. She zippered her jacket all the way up to her throat and trust her hands into her pockets. She looked at her mother inquisitively. What were they doing here? Linda's expression revealed nothing since she was unsure herself.

They stared at the front of the school. It was a two story brick building with a central entrance way and wings that expanded in both directions. A series of long and short windows ran the length of each wing. Nicole gazed at the school. Then slightly annoyed at this game, she turned to her mother asked again, "What are we doing here, Mom?"

"I'm really not sure," Linda said. "Someone from the school called and asked me to take you down here and told me to park right here."

All at once there was movement in some windows. Nicole

noticed waving hands. In the next instant students occupied each window throughout the school front. They were waving to Nicole. Then, when they knew they had Nicole's attention, they began to hold up signs. WE MISS YOU, NICOLE!! GET WELL SOON!! HURRY BACK!! WE LOVE YOU, NICOLE!! IT'S NOT THE SAME WITHOUT YOU!!

Linda was immediately in tears. Nicole was laughing and crying at the same time. She was waving to her friends and even kids she didn't know. Then she saw her close friends, Sam and Emily and Ashley and all the others. They had their faces pressed up to the windows trying to make Nicole laugh. She waved to them and made silly faces back at them.

Then the principal came to the door and waved for Linda to come inside. At first Linda shook her head no, but he continued to wave his hand in a beckoning motion. "Go, Mom," Nicole told her. When she went in, there were so many teachers there who hugged her and cried with her and wished Nicole and her well. Nicole was still outside waving to her friends and laughing at their silly antics. When her mom came out of the school, she was carrying a big box. As she approached the car with it, Nicole asked, "What's all that?"

"These are all signs and cards that your friends and classmates and teachers made for you. There are some wrapped gifts here. Everyone was so wonderful." Linda was crying. "They care for you so much," she told her daughter as she handed Nicole a bunch of cards and placed the box of gifts and signs in the trunk. "We better get going. I don't think you should be out much longer," Linda stated.

Nicole turned to the school and made one more series of enthusiastic waves to everyone. She blew kisses to her friends and pounded a fist to her heart. Her friends responded likewise.

Then she was in the car and Nicole and Linda were pulling away, heading back to a world of isolation and the harsh reality that in another week she would have to go back to the hospital for a second stem cell transplant.

Sitting in the passenger seat, she read the cards and the notes. Tears filled her eyes at some of the messages. Others made her laugh. Then the car pulled into the driveway at 355 East 12th Street. Linda carried the box and they walked into the house. Looking at the box's contents, they both realized that Nicole might have to stay in isolation for a while, but she would never be alone. Her friends in Northampton would always be with her in her thoughts.

Chapter Six

Nicole was only home a few days and then it was Halloween. Already bored and lonely from the drudgery of being stuck in her house that so few could enter, Nicole's spirits were lifted on Halloween night when all of her friends and the neighborhood kids came Trick or Treating. Doug set himself up outside on the porch so he could provide all of Trick or Treaters with candy. More importantly, however, Doug also had a walkie-talkie with him and had given Nicole the other one to keep with her inside the house. When her friends came to the house, Nicole was able to wave at them through the window and talk with them on the walkie-talkies. Over the course of the night, Nicole was able to talk with all of her closest friends and any well wishers who came by. Throughout the course of the night, there was a steady stream of people who were excited and eager to speak with Nicole. Her friends joked with her and made faces at her, which she returned through the window. Nicole laughed hysterically at their antics and costumes. It had been a long time since she had laughed like that. The time flew by. But then the number of visitors dwindled in their steadiness and finally, as the evening wore on and the time for Trick or Treating expired, Nicole realized she was back to being alone, back in isolation.

After two weeks, it was time for Nicole to return to CHOP for the second stem cell transplant. It was something that Nicole knew was necessary, but was dreading nonetheless. The doctors were always upfront with her about what to expect with each procedure. They pulled no punches this time in letting her know that as bad as she thought the first procedure's effects were, the second one was going to be even worse.

Once again Nicole disagreed with the timetable the doctors laid out for her. "This procedure will keep you in the hospital for about four weeks," the doctors told her.

"No way," Nicole rebuked. "I'm not spending Thanksgiving in the hospital. I'll be home in two weeks. I'll be home for Thanksgiving."

The doctors were a bit more skeptical this time. They knew what Nicole was in for. This time Nicole was given three days of intense chemotherapy. This was followed by three days of full body radiation. This caused her skin to darken because, in essence, she was being burned from within. Later, when her friends would see photos of Nicole from this time period, they would comment about the great tan she had. Nicole assured them it was not a tan and that they really wouldn't want to have to go through what she did in order to get their skin that tone.

The side effects of the radiation were even worse this time on Nicole. The vomiting was incessant and more violent than she ever experienced. It wreaked havoc on her insides to the point that in one vicious bout, her stomach lining was ripped apart, and when she threw up, that came up too. What made the vomiting even worse were the open sores in her mouth. As the bile and other bodily fluids passed over them, Nicole convulsed in paroxysms of pain.

In between bouts of nausea, Nicole tried to carry on as normal. She even went on Ebay and bought her father a Penn State University poster for Christmas. "Still doesn't stop you from spending, does it?" Linda joked with her daughter. But Nicole could barely talk, the sores in her throat and mouth burned so badly. Once again, the ICEE drinks were the only things that soothed the pain for a little while. As the days wore on, the mucousitis returned and Nicole had to once again deal with this paste-like substance constantly oozing from her body.

She was on morphine to dull the pain, but she had an allergic reaction to it and began to scratch at herself to the point where she was creating open sores on her skin. The doctors had to put gloves on her to prevent her from doing more external harm to herself.

The days were long and unpleasant. She kept in contact with her friends through the computer, but aside from her parents, no one was allowed to visit. Once, she and Linda were able to pass a few hours looking out the hospital window onto 34th street as Ben Afleck was filming a new movie down below. But other than that, very few events broke up the monotony and life in her hospital room.

Linda never let Nicole sleep alone. Every time she was in the hospital, Linda stayed with Nicole constantly. She slept in her room and was Nicole's best nurse. Doug would arrive each day around 4:00 PM after spending the day at school. He would go home around 11:00 each night to do laundry. The most important items he would bring back each day were clean sheets and blankets for Nicole, who insisted on having her own bed linen from home.

One night, Linda was awakened from her sleep by a horrific scream. It had come from someone in the room next door. It was a sound unlike any Linda had ever heard. There was a dreadfulness in the shriek that went right through Linda. She rose immediately. She checked on Nicole, who, under heavy medication, didn't hear the lamenting wail. She then went to her door and listened to the quick footsteps of the hospital staff making their way to the girl in the next room. She continued to hear the girl's mother moaning and sobbing. When she realized what was happening, she knew she needed to call her husband. Even though it was the middle of the night she was shaken so much that she needed to talk to him. "Doug," she started, and then broke down and cried. "Doug, the girl in the room next door just passed away. She died Doug. She just celebrated her 17th birthday and she died."

Nicole was released from CHOP the day before Thanksgiving. She continued to amaze doctors with her resolve and resiliency. She was a battler. She had all the attributes of a survivor.

She did suffer a minor setback the day after Thanksgiving when her blood cell numbers dropped below acceptable levels. She only had to go to the Lehigh Valley hospital to be monitored and was back home in just a few days. At home, she was back to a life of isolation. She was quarantined from the world again in an effort to reduce her risk of contracting an infection. December and Christmas came and went and the tedious boredom of a life with little human contact began to take its toll on Nicole. Doug and Linda watched helplessly as Nicole slipped into depression. She began to resist medication and to lose her appetite. She also began to lose a bit of her positive outlook and determination.

The Sheriffs went to see Dr. Monteleone. After meeting with Nicole, Dr. Monteleone thought that Nicole was in need of an antidepressant. But Nicole was adamantly opposed to the idea. "I've heard my dad talk about the dangers of using drugs and I'm not about to use them," Nicole argued.

"Nicole," Dr. Monteleone said to her, "I give you credit for making it this far without an antidepressant. Most kids who have to go through what you have gone through are on something long before this period. You lasted longer than most without a drug to help you. But now you need something to keep you going."

All of those times she heard her father give speeches at his school to other kids about the dangers of drugs. In their very open father-daughter talks, Doug always preached to Nicole about how she needed to live a life free from the influence of drugs. And now here was a doctor telling her she needed to take drugs to lift her spirits? She couldn't understand the mixed messages. She wouldn't allow it, and so her parents let it go for the time being.

In late January she developed a fever that just wouldn't go away. Finally, her Lehigh Valley doctors order her to take an ambulance back down to CHOP. Back at CHOP, she was placed in a room that had no windows and she began to fall deeper and deeper into depression.

Finally, Linda called Sue Carlson. "Sue, we could really use your help," Linda told her. "Nicole's fallen into a depression we can't get her out of. She won't eat, she's lethargic, and she's lost a little bit of her fight. If you can swing it, we could really use your help with Nicole. I think she really needs to talk to someone like you."

Sue didn't hesitate to say yes. She was in her car driving down to CHOP within the hour. Once she got there, she was greeted by Doug and Linda, who offered their impressions of Nicole's state of mind. Sue listened intently and then said, "I'm not making any promises I'll be able to change anything," she said. "But I'll do my best to try and get her to talk." With that, she entered Nicole's room.

Sue just had this effect on Nicole that allowed Nicole to open up and reveal her inner most feelings. She was close with her parents and shared almost all of her thoughts and feelings with them. But they were her parents. There were some things children never want to share with their parents, no matter how good the relationship is. And Nicole was no different. In addition, there were some thoughts she was protecting her parents from. With Sue, Nicole was able to be open and frank about her thoughts. She didn't have to worry about hurting her, or even worse, frightening her, with her thoughts. So for the next four hours she opened up to her school counselor and revealed her inner most thoughts, her own fears, her own visions of the future. She revealed her dreams and her nightmares.

When Sue came out of the room, she agreed with Dr. Monteleone; Nicole was definitely in a deep state of depression and was definitely incapable of pulling herself out of it. She was in need of medication. Fortunately, Sue also got Nicole to agree to take an antidepressant drug on the terms that she could stop taking them once she felt herself again. The Sheriffs couldn't thank Sue enough for the time she had just spent with their daughter.

The next day, the doctor explained to Nicole that he was prescribing Marinol for her. He said that Marinol was a derivative of marijuana and it would help lift Nicole's spirits and get her out of her depressed state. When Nicole heard the explanation, she started to emphatically shake her head back and forth and stated very definitively that she wasn't going to take *that* drug. "I'm not taking marijuana. I agreed to take medicine, not drugs. My father has always said that I should say no to drugs. Well, I'm saying no now. I'm not taking anything with pot in it!"

Linda had to call Doug at school. "*Your* daughter is at it again. She won't take the Marinol because they told her it contains marijuana. I think you need to come down here and explain the difference. She won't listen to anyone else."

Doug drove down immediately. When he got to her room he was greeted by an angry scowl. "What's wrong, Sweet Pea?" he asked her.

"You know what's wrong. They want me to take a drug with marijuana in it and I don't think I should. I'm not taking it."

"Sweet Pea, I know you always listened to my talks to the other kids. But remember, I was always talking about illegal drugs. When kids buy pot on the street and smoke it, that's illegal and has no good use. But when doctors prescribe it for medicinal purposes, that's okay. Honey, I wouldn't let you take it if it wasn't good for you. It's a medicine. It will help you to start eating. It'll help you to feel yourself again. Okay?"

Nicole nodded. That day she began to take her Marinol.

A few days later, Nicole developed an infection around the opening of her broviac tube. The doctors decided that since Nicole was through with her chemotherapy, they could take it out. "What do you think, Nicole?" the doctor asked. "If we take it out, then you can actually become a little more active. You can even shoot some hoops." This brightened Nicole more than anything and she agreed to let them remove the tube right then and there. She held Linda's hand as the doctor's unstitched the zipper they had created in her chest. Then, as Nicole held her breath, she watched as the doctor eased the tube out of the hole and waved it in display. Nicole breathed deeply with relief.

Once the infection was under control, Nicole was able to go home. The Sheriffs developed a routine of eating breakfast together before Doug would go off to school. Nicole was still stuck in a homebound isolation. She passed the days keeping up with her schoolwork and writing in her journal. Linda maintained the house and looked after Nicole, making sure that she properly took her medications.

One morning, Doug was eating a bowl of cereal with blueberries. He noticed a blueberry that had fallen out of the bowl and nonchalantly picked it up and tossed it back into the bowl. Nicole then sat down to join him at the table. As the father and daughter were talking Linda walked by and surveyed the table.

"Did you take your Marinol?" she asked Nicole.

"You didn't give it to me yet," Nicole responded.

"Yes I did. I left it right there on the table."

"Mom, I would have seen it if you left it here. It's not here."

Just then Doug finished the last grains of cereal in his bowl and placed his spoon down. "That was good," he said. "I love cereal and blueberries."

"Dad, did you see my Marinol?" Nicole asked him.

"No, I didn't. You sure you put it out, Linda?"

"I know I put it out right next to where you're sitting."

"What color is the Marinol pill?" Doug asked.

"It's purple," Linda said. "It's about the size of a small pea."

Doug looked into his bowl. Then he looked at Linda and Nicole. "Could it be mistaken for a blueberry? I picked up what I thought was a blueberry and threw it in my bowl."

Linda looked into his empty bowl. "Doug, you ate Nicole's Marinol!" Nicole howled with laughter. Linda was dumbfounded and wondered what effect the pill would have on her husband. When Doug got to school, he told his secretary Diane the whole

story. Then he went directly to Curt, his principal, and explained
to him how he thought he might be under the influence of
marijuana this morning. There were two ironies to the situation.
The first was that Doug had never taken an illegal drug in his
entire life. The second was that some people liked him better
under the drug's influence. His secretary secretly called Linda and
told her how calm Doug was that day. "He's so mellow," Diane
told Linda. "You got any more of those things for him? If I were
you, I'd order a case of them!" Both women laughed. Nicole
would be sure to tell the tale to every doctor they had to see over
the next two weeks.

The change in his demeanor because of the drug's influence
actually enlightened Doug to something he hadn't seen before. He
had thought he was doing well. He thought he was the same guy
he always was at school. He had always been quick to make a joke
or pull a prank on a colleague. He had always been an omnipresent
athletic director, at every event on every day. He prided himself on
being an athletic director who knew all the players in his athletic
programs and who was deemed to be approachable by his coaches.
What he didn't realize was that he had changed. He wasn't the same
man. He didn't understand that he never could be the same man.
But he was often angry now and frustrated. When he saw his student
athletes carrying on normal lives, he couldn't help but to feel bitter
inside. He had thought he was masking all of this, but it showed. His
good friends, like Curt and Diane dealt with it, other colleagues just
stayed away. They didn't know what to say to him. But on the day
he was under the influence of Marinol, the difference in his mental
disposition was evident to those who were closest to him.

After the first few weeks of February, it was apparent the Marinol was improving Nicole's state of mind but was not helping to alleviate her weight loss problem. A year ago, Nicole was a muscular 119 pounds. Now she was a frail 94 pounds and growing weaker. She just couldn't seem to gain weight. It wasn't that she wasn't trying. In fact, she consumed about 10,000 calories a day. But her body just wasn't capable yet of holding the weight. As a result, during her next visit to the doctors, they decided she would need a feeding tube. Nicole was vehemently against it. She pleaded and cried hysterically to her father. "Daddy, don't let them do this to me. I don't want it. Don't make me have to wear tubes coming out of my nose. I'll eat more. I promise. Just don't let them put that in me."

Doug was shaken by his daughter's plea. He was considering the impact that wearing this tube all of the time might have on her mental state. But she was 94 pounds and dropping. He knew it had to be done. He was crying himself when he told her, "Sweet Pea, it has to be done. We don't have any other choice. You know the doctors only do what's best for you. You need to add weight to get your strength back. Then we'll be able to shoot some hoops together again. It'll only be for a little while until you start to gain weight on your own."

All the while Doug was trying to convince her, Nicole was shaking her head. The tears hadn't stopped flowing. But at last Nicole realized she wasn't going to win this battle with her dad and the doctors. She reluctantly relented and allowed them to install a tube up through her nose and down her throat. The tube coming out of her nose was taped to her face and coiled around her ear. At night time, a bag holding a nutrient rich concoction was attached to the tube and the fluid dripped into Nicole's body while she slept.

Nicole was allowed a few visitors at home now. When they came into the house, they had to scrub their hands and put on surgical masks. Nicole was so happy when her friends would stop by. It broke up the monotony of her dull daily life. When her friends came to visit, she would immediately perk up and Doug and Linda would witness a glimmer of the vibrancy and giddiness that had always been their daughter's trademark. Nicole would welcome her guests by drawing funny noses and mouths on their surgical masks.

As promised, Doug began to allow Nicole to shoot baskets. He would bring Nicole down to his school when no one was around and they would shoot hoops together. Nicole would complain about her loss of stamina and skills, but Doug would just marvel at the fact that he and his daughter were once again doing what they had always loved to do best. Linda chastised him for bringing Nicole to school, but he assured her no one else was around. "Besides, it's great just to see her happy and active again."

Sometimes she would get too active. Then her feeding tube would aggravate her stomach and Nicole would throw up. The tube would come up her nose and out of her mouth. Linda would have to pull the whole thing out. Doug just couldn't bring himself to do it. He thought he would hurt his daughter. And so it became a ritual that Doug and Nicole would go play basketball, Nicole would come home and throw up, and Linda would pull out the complete tubing apparatus. Then they would have to go to the hospital to have a new tube inserted.

On one occasion, the Sheriffs called the hospital to let the doctors know Nicole was on her way to get a new feeding tube. Dr. Stern happened to be on duty and she said she would wait for the Sheriffs before she went home. However, on this night, the Sheriffs were uncharacteristically late in getting to the hospital.

When they arrived, Dr. Stern inquired, "What took you so long? I've been waiting for you."

Nicole said, "My mother had to wash her hair."

Dr. Stern showed a slight hint of being perturbed. "I wish I had the time to wash my hair when people were waiting for me," she said.

"Well my mom *had* to wash her hair," Nicole stated. "When she was pulling out my feeding tube, I threw up on her head. She was kneeling in front of me as she was pulling the hose out of my nose and I threw up right on her. It was a direct shot!"

Dr. Stern laughed hysterically. "Give me five," she told Nicole and they high fived each other.

The only breaks Nicole had in her tedious home routine were her trips to the gym with her dad and visits to doctors' offices. February was long, dreary, and lonely. Her friends would call or stop by on occasion, they would IM and email each other, but for the most part, Nicole was alone. As March began, and she began to add weight, she made up her mind about what she wanted to do. On her next visits to Dr. Stern and Dr. Monteleone she let them know her intentions. "It's time for me to get back to normal," she told them. "It's time for me to get back to school."

Dr. Stern wasn't sure that would be a good medical decision. "You know, you're not supposed to go back until September. That's when we thought you would be in the clear."

"I know that, but I really want to go back. I'm tired of being home and being alone. I don't feel like I'm a sick person anymore. I just want to be normal again," Nicole explained.

"I'll tell you what," Dr. Stern said. "You have an appointment next week with Dr. Bunin at CHOP. If she clears you to go back to school, I will too." Dr. Bunin was the stem cell specialist at CHOP who performed Nicole's stem cell transplants. Nicole smiled and hugged Dr. Stern.

When she met with Dr. Bunin the following week, the doctor performed a complete examination and went over Nicole's blood test results. She was happy with what she saw. "So, Dr. Stern tells me you made a request to her. What is it that you want to do?"

"I want to go back to school. I'm bored. I feel fine. I want to finish eighth grade and be with my friends," Nicole told her.

"And what kind of time table did you have in mind?" she asked Nicole. "When do you want to go back?"

"I want to go back to school on April 14th. That's my birthday," she told her.

Dr. Bunin was impressed that Nicole had already thought this all out. She realized how important this was to her patient.

"I'll make you a deal. If you can get your weight up and we can get rid of the feeding tube, I'll clear you to go back to school on April 14th," Dr. Bunning offered.

Nicole smiled and shook the doctor's hand. "It's a deal," Nicole said.

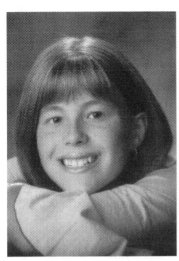

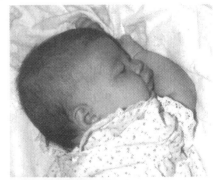

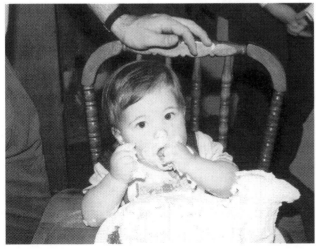

Chapter Seven

W hile most teenagers loathe the thought of being in school seven hours a day, five days a week, Nicole was anxiously looking forward to it. She couldn't wait to get to school. She couldn't wait to see all of her friends and to go to classes together. Her parents and Sue Carlson were coordinating her re-entry back into school life. Sue met with the teachers to discuss how to best help Nicole re-acclimate herself to the school environment after having been away from it for most of the school year.

The week before Nicole was set to start, a local newspaper ran an article about Nicole and her battle with Ewing sarcoma. In it, Nicole said, "I put my faith in the Lord. He guided me." She never lost faith. She never wavered in her conviction that she would defeat the disease. She admitted in the article that she had learned to appreciate things more: things like shooting baskets without throwing up, being able to run and open the door when the doorbell rang, and having too much homework. She constantly looked forward to what was ahead of her. She saw that the future was filled with opportunities, and she firmly believed she would be able to live out her dreams. In the article she stated:

"I think I'm going to study medicine so I can become a doctor and help other people."

It had been almost a year ago when she was diagnosed with cancer. But now it was April 14th, 2003: her fourteenth birthday. She was two weeks removed from her feeding tube. Her doctors had declared her cancer in remission. There was a car filled with friends waiting in the driveway. And just as she had predicted, Nicole Sheriff was going back to school!

Stephanie's mom was driving and Nicole slipped into the seat next to her in the front, just as she had done back in September. Nicole and her friends had called their seats back in September when school first started. On the way to school on the last day Nicole attended back in October, Nicole turned around in her seat and looked at her friends. She looked at Ashley and said, "Now, Ash, even though I'm not going to be here, don't let anyone sit in my seat. I'll be back." Ashley nodded. Stephanie nodded as well. As they were driving to school on Nicole's first day back, Nicole turned around from the front seat and thanked them for remaining true to their words.

As Nicole made her way to her locker, she was greeted by one elated scream after another as her friends ecstatically expressed their happiness at seeing Nicole again. She hugged and kissed everyone as she made her way to her locker. When she got to it, she saw it was decorated with balloons and ribbons and "Welcome Back" signs. She made it through the day with a perpetual smile on her face.

On Friday night, Nicole was lured to her friend Brittany's house, unaware that most of her girl friends and most of the field hockey team were hiding in the basement. When Nicole hit the last step into the basement, her friends yelled, "Surprise!" They then began to sing "Happy Birthday" to Nicole. They spent the rest of the night raucously celebrating the return of their friend. They danced crazily and sang at the top of their lungs to their favorite songs. They called boys on their cell phones. Nicole got Brittany to call Ben on Brittany's phone. Nicole and Ben admitted to each other that they still liked each other a lot. The party went on until almost midnight.

When all of their energy was spent, the girls collapsed onto the couch and into chairs and onto the floor. They held each other and rested against each other's backs and on each other's folded legs. It was girl talk time, a time when they allowed themselves to actually express their true feelings or admit things they did or things they didn't know. They didn't look at each other. They just talked while looking at the ceiling or with their eyes closed. In this calm openness, Ashley asked Nicole a question many of them had been thinking to themselves: "Are you ever afraid it's going to come back?" Nicole didn't make eye contact with anyone. She was lying on the floor with her hands interlocked under her head. She spoke to the ceiling. "The doctors say only about 10 percent of the people who have this cancer the way I had it survive. I'm going to be in that 10 percent. I'm going to beat this thing." They were all scared for her. They had been scared ever since Nicole was first diagnosed. But Nicole calmed those fears, and when she told them she was going to beat the disease, they believed her.

As the school year wound down, Nicole had fully immersed herself back into it as much as possible. She ran for and won the position of class vice president. It was a position in which she was to serve all of freshmen year. She also started to help some adults coach the elementary school basketball teams. The kids all knew about her and knew her story. She would use this time not just to teach basketball but also to talk about the disease to her players and teach them about how they should act if one of their friends ever got sick.

There was only one limitation put on Nicole, and it was the hardest one to accept. When her doctors originally told Nicole her cancer was in remission, she immediately dreamed about playing basketball and field hockey with her friends. But then her doctors had to deliver the bad news to her. "You won't be able to play basketball or field hockey," Dr. Stern told her. "At least not for a long time."

"What do you mean?" Nicole asked incredulously. "I'm an athlete. I'm a field hockey and basketball player. That's what I do."

"Yes," Dr. Stern agreed, but then she went on to explain to Nicole why she couldn't compete in any sports where there was the potential for contact. "But right now, your bones are so brittle. All the treatments you've had in the past year have taken their toll on the strength of your bones. Right now, they are just too brittle for you to take a chance that the contact that happens during those sports will not happen. If you happen to be hit during a game or practice, you'd end up right back in ICU. Your bone would break like shatterproof glass."

Nicole sat in a stunned silence. This was something that she had not been prepared for. She always assumed that once the cancer was in remission, it would be time to get back to a normal life. That's what the doctors had always told her. And now they were telling her that she couldn't play anymore. Well that wasn't her definition of normal. Normal for Nicole was playing basketball and field hockey at break-neck speed. It meant being uninhibited about crashing into someone or diving for a loose ball on the floor.

In addition to the playing restrictions, Nicole would have to have MRI's performed on her every three months to make sure the cancer was not coming back.

"Well, I guess I only have one choice for a sport this summer and next fall," she said. The doctors and her parents looked at her inquisitively. "I'll go out for tennis. There's no contact there."

They were all amazed once again at her resiliency. Here she was, a 14-year-old girl whose life-long passions had just been taken away. But she didn't let that set her back. She refused to let this bother her and had all ready come up with a contingency plan. Nicole was ready to begin practicing for a sport that she never really played. But she knew she needed to be playing something. She would never be able to handle not playing a sport at all. She was too competitive and had too much energy. The doctors and her parents agreed that it was a good plan.

The Sheriffs were also able to do something that summer they had been unable to do the year before; they went on vacation. They made the drive to the New Jersey shore town of Wildwood and spent a week on the beach and boardwalk. They went out to fancy restaurants and shopped. In Doug's mind, it was the best vacation he had ever been on. He had his wife and healthy daughter with him and that was all he had ever wanted. Outside of the Lobster House restaurant, there is a harbor where the fishing boats coming in from the Atlantic Ocean unload their catches of the day. As the Sheriffs waited for their name to be called on the restaurant's outside speaker system, Linda told Nicole and Doug to pose while standing in front of a trawler. It was only when they got home and developed the photo that they noticed the name of the ship: My Girl. It instantly became Doug's favorite photo. Many times in the upcoming months he would stare at their smiling faces and see how happy they both were. He thought that their embrace somehow captured the love they had for each other. Nicole seemed so healthy in the photo, so vibrant and full of life. Looking at it, one would never have guessed what was in store in Nicole's immediate future.

———

When they returned home from the shore, Linda scheduled Nicole's first MRI. As she did, she realized how quickly three months had passed and how easily it was to take days for granted. She knew Nicole was a bit nervous about the upcoming test and so she decided to take her and a friend out shopping. Nicole chose to take Krista. She was always someone who made Nicole laugh. But Nicole didn't laugh that much that day as they shopped the mall. Krista noticed that her friend was rather sullen and withdrawn. It was while they were eating dinner when Krista overheard what was on her friend's mind.

After shopping, Linda decided to take them to a local Ruby Tuesday's restaurant. After they had ordered, there was a lull in their conversation. Krista saw Nicole lean over and begin to whisper to her mother. But Krista heard the words and they sent a shiver through her body. "Mommy, I have a weird feeling it's back," Nicole confessed to her mother. The three of them barely touched their food after it arrived.

The next day, Nicole had the MRI done, and two days after that, she and her parents went to Dr. Stern's office together to learn what the images revealed. It was June 30, 2003. Nicole sat on her father's lap as they awaited Dr. Stern's arrival into the office.

Dr. Stern sat across from the family and looked them in the eyes. She was not one for small talk when there were important issues at hand. She also always got straight to the point. This time the point stung so hard that it seemed to deflate Nicole right before their eyes. "Our tests revealed a mass on Nicole's spine," she said flatly. "There's another tumor." Nicole immediately burst into tears. Both of here parents didn't even bother to wipe the tears running from their own eyes and down their cheeks. As Dr. Stern went on to discuss treatment options, Nicole got up and started heading for the door.

"Nicole. Where are you going?" Linda called. "Nicole..." But her daughter never turned around. She threw open the door and quickly exited into the medical center's hallway. Linda got up to go after her, but Doug put his hand on his wife's lap and convinced her not to follow Nicole.

"Let her go," Doug said. "Just let her be by herself and cry it out. She's an athlete who just lost a battle. She just lost a game. It's a typical response of an athlete."

Linda looked at her husband questioningly. He nodded assuredly to her, confident he knew what he was talking about. There was a long silence in the room as Linda fought the urge to go after her daughter. Finally Doug said, "It's an athlete's way of responding to bad results. But don't worry. She'll bounce back. She always does."

The Sheriffs finished the consultation with the doctor and made plans for Nicole to begin treatments immediately. They left the office and went to the car where they found Nicole already in the back seat. Her eyes were swollen and red, but the tears appeared to be finished. The family drove a while in silence. Finally Nicole broke the silence. "You know what," she started in such a loud voice that she startled both of her parents in the front seats. Doug looked at his daughter in the rear view mirror. She was staring out the window. He sensed a competitive edge to her voice and knew the game was back on. "I am NOT going to be a statistic to this cancer. I REFUSE to become a statistic to this cancer." She was still staring out the window. She was shaking her head back and forth. "I'm going to prove them all wrong," she promised. "They're all wrong. I am NOT going to be a statistic." Linda and Doug nodded in agreement at their daughter's conviction.

<hr>

When she got home, she went on the Internet and began to peruse various cancer related websites. On the St. Jude Children's Hospital site, she saw a number for people to call to consult with a doctor. She decided to give it a try. Doug heard her dialing, but decided to keep his distance from her activities. He eavesdropped instead.

When her call was answered, Nicole began: "Hi, I'd like to talk to you about a patient who was diagnosed with Ewing sarcoma a year and a half ago and has gone through several stages of treatments." Nicole rattled off the chemotherapies she had been through and gave details about the stem cells harvests and transplants. Finally she provided the doctor on the other side of the call information regarding the most current tests she's been through and the details about her most recent diagnosis.

"How old is the patient?" the doctor asked.

"Fourteen," Nicole said.

"What's her name?"

"Nicole," she stated, a bit puzzled.

"Is she your daughter?" the doctor asked.

"No, I'm Nicole. The patient is me."

"You're only 14?" the doctor asked.

"Yes, but I'm pretty mature for my age."

"I'll say," the doctor said. "Nicole, I'll need to talk with a parent if I can."

"Sure, my father's right here," she said, and Doug sheepishly made his way into the room, knowing his daughter was aware of him listening all along.

"Hello, this is Doug Sheriff."

"Mr. Sheriff this is Dr. Johnson of St. Jude Children's Hospital in Tennessee. I guess you know that your daughter called here."

"She did that on her own, Doctor."

"Mr. Sheriff. Is she really only 14 years old?"

"That's correct, Doctor."

"Well, she's amazing. I was so impressed with her knowledge and understanding of all those medications and procedures. I really thought I was talking to the patient's mother."

"That's Nicole. We are so proud of how well she advocates for herself," Doug confessed. His voice had been cheery, but then it turned serious when he asked, "What do you think of what she's gone through, Doctor? Is there anything you would be doing differently?"

"Nicole said you are dealing with a Dr. Stern. Have her contact me tomorrow and we'll discuss some possible options for Nicole. It sounds to me like they've used all the appropriate protocols so far. Maybe we can help with some ideas for this next series of treatments."

The Sheriffs were back in Dr. Stern's office the next day. When Dr. Stern entered, Nicole got up and handed her Dr. Johnson's name and number. "Here you go," she said to Dr. Stern. "I went on line last night and got in touch with a doctor at St. Jude Children's Hospital in Tennessee. You're supposed to contact this doctor today."

Dr. Stern was taken aback. Doug felt a bit guilty and explained, "It was her idea, Dr. Stern. She did this all on her own."

Dr. Stern looked at them all. "That's fine with me. If you think this displeases me, you're mistaken. Like I've been telling you all along, if you hear of anything or read about anything that you think will help us, you bring it in to me. We'll investigate it. I have no problem with that whatsoever."

Dr. Stern did call Dr. Johnson. They discussed Nicole's case in detail, starting from when she was initially diagnosed. They reviewed the specifics of all of the treatments and went over the latest test results. Dr. Johnson gave Dr. Stern an update on some of the new procedures and medicines the doctors at St. Jude's were using and having some success with. They then debated which would be the best way to treat Nicole's tumor. Dr. Johnson first suggested surgery to remove the tumor, but Dr. Stern thought that there was too much risk in that considering that the tumor was attached to the spine. They decided on a new drug that St. Jude's was using specifically to treat Ewing sarcoma. It was an oral chemotherapy drug.

Dr. Stern figured out the maximum amount Nicole's body could handle. The potential options for treating Nicole were somewhat limited this time around. Since the doctors had opted for such a strong and aggressive approach the year before, Nicole's body would only be able to tolerate certain treatments now. Radiation was not an option because of the amount that Nicole had been exposed to over the last year. And so Dr. Stern prescribed this oral chemotherapy drug in the hope that it would slow down the tumor's growth rate and prevent other tumors from developing.

So as July wore on, Nicole would take her chemo orally and then go off and attend voluntary tennis practices two days a week. She quickly learned her body was not what it used to be. When she would come home from the practices, she was totally exhausted. She would immediately go to sleep for four hours in order to recover from the workouts. At times her blood counts dropped dangerously low. When this happened, she had to be taken into the doctor's office immediately. Throughout July her counts fluctuated so much that Nicole now required blood transfusions.

At night time, whenever she was able, she would head up to the town pool and hang out with her friends and talk to the boys, who were never far from her thoughts.

A white limo pulled up to the Sheriff house. Nicole ran out excitedly to greet it. "It's here!" she screamed. "It's here!" The driver loaded up the Sheriffs' suitcases and soon they were on their way to Newark Airport where the Sheriffs would hop a plane to Florida so Nicole could begin her Dream Come True vacation. Dream Come True is an organization that sponsors vacations and special events for young cancer victims. When Nicole was asked where she dreamed about going on her dream vacation, she immediately said she wanted to swim with the dolphins in Sea World and walk down Main Street in Disney World. Her wishes were granted. The family was to stay at the Yacht Club in Disney World and spend five days enjoying the Orlando area attractions.

On the first full day there, Nicole spent the morning swimming with the dolphins in Sea World. She was amazed at their beauty and intelligence. A comfort came over her body as she petted the backs of the friendly sea mammals. Her love for these animals was forever captured in a photo of Nicole bending gently over a dolphin ready to kiss it on the back of its head.

That afternoon, the Sheriffs headed for Disney's Epcot Theme Park. The late July sun bore down on the family as Doug pushed Nicole around the park in a wheelchair. The combination of the oral chemo medication and the sun severely weakened Nicole. The mid afternoon temperature was around 98 degrees, and yet Nicole couldn't get rid of a chill that had entered her body. She had felt the chill when she had gotten out of the water that morning and attributed the lingering chill to the air conditioning at the hotel. But now, as the sun scorched those around her, Nicole was seeking to contain the chill by wearing an oversized sweatshirt and wrapping herself in a blanket. Neither was working as she began to shiver uncontrollably. Her arms were trembling and her lips were quivering as the family waited in the handicap line for the boat that would take them back to the Yacht Club.

Linda felt Nicole's forehead. "Doug, she's burning up." She felt Nicole's wrist and the back of her neck. Nicole's teeth were chattering. A look of panic came over Linda as Nicole closed her eyes and moaned. Doug shaded his eyes as he looked off in the distance at the arriving boat.

Just then a gentleman who had been watching the family stepped towards them. He looked at Linda. "Is there a problem here, mam?" he asked. "I'm with Disney security. Is everything alright?"

Doug quickly explained Nicole's predicament to the gentlemen.

"It looks like your daughter needs medical attention," the man said. He turned his head and began to speak into a microphone that was housed on his shoulder. He reported his location and said that he was in need of a medical team immediately. Within five minutes a speedboat came whipping around the dock and glided right up onto the landing. All at once, the crew was out and tending to Nicole. Within minutes they had assessed that she had a temperature of 104 and was dehydrated. She was taken from her wheel chair and placed on a stretcher that had been rolled out of an ambulance that had just arrived.

As Doug and Linda were providing the medical team with more information regarding Nicole's illness, the Disney characters of Cinderella and Prince Charming appeared and made their way over to Nicole. Prince charming bent over and kissed Nicole's hand. Cinderella held Nicole's hand and then kissed her on the cheek, leaving lip marks on the side of Nicole's face. Soon other Disney characters came and wished Nicole well as her stretcher was rolled into the ambulance. Once inside, the attending medic pulled out a stuffed Dalmatian and gave it to Nicole to hold on to. Within ten minutes of informing the security guard that their daughter was not feeling well, Nicole was on her way to Celebration Hospital.

At the Celebration Hospital, the doctors worked to get Nicole's temperature down and to get her blood pressure to rise. But the temperature held and the blood pressure kept falling. After seven hours, she was stable enough to be transported to Orlando Children's Hospital. Once here, Doug was able to get in touch with Dr. Monteleone and Dr. Stern and apprise them of Nicole's condition. The doctors in Pennsylvania emailed all of Nicole's medical charts to the doctors in Florida. Soon the doctors were able to get Nicole blood transfusions. As the night wore on, her blood counts began to rise and it appeared that Nicole was on the road to recovery.

In her weakened state, Nicole was in no condition to travel. The doctors anticipated it would be at least a week before she was well enough to get out of the hospital. As she always did in hospitals, Linda stayed right by Nicole's side. Doug was transported back and forth from the hospital to the hotel in a van which Disney World provided.

On the third night, when Doug arrived back at the hotel, there was a message on his room phone for him to report to the front desk. He immediately made his way there, nervously expecting to hear some bad news.

"Hi. I'm Doug Sheriff. I had a message for me to report here," Doug said to the woman behind the desk.

She smiled warmly at him. "How are you, Mr. Sheriff? We heard what your daughter's been going through. We're really sorry."

"Thanks so much," Doug said to her. "Everyone's been so great to us."

"So Nicole only got to spend one day in Disney before she got sick?" the woman asked.

"Yeah," Doug began to explain. "We were in Epcott on the afternoon of our first day when everything started to happen."

"And this was supposed to be her Dream Come True vacation, right?"

"Yeah, some dream," Doug said sarcastically. "More like a nightmare."

"Well here's what Disney World wants to do, Mr. Sheriff. When Nicole gets out of the hospital, if she's well enough, we'd like to extend her vacation for five more days. On us," she added.

"I don't know how to thank you," Doug said, taken aback by the demonstration of concern and compassion.

"We just hope she gets better soon," the woman said. Then she reached down under the desk and pulled out a stuffed Winnie the Pooh and handed it to Doug. "Can you give this to her and tell her to get better?" the woman asked.

"I sure will," Doug said moving away, dazed by the kindness.

After five days, Nicole was released from Orlando Hospital and the Sheriffs enjoyed five more days of fun at the various Disney theme parks. It was a time the Sheriffs all cherished immensely.

Chapter Eight

Deb Anthony first heard about this girl named Nicole Sheriff from the middle school coaches. The coaches often spoke about this girl who had been a wonderful athlete who was now battling cancer. One of the reasons why Deb was such a successful high school field hockey coach was because she genuinely showed an interest in her players' lives. She was not just a coach, but she was also a leader, a teacher, and a role model. Because she cared so much about her players, her players worked so hard not to let her down. The last thing they wanted to do was disappoint Coach Anthony. She wasn't a woman who was just interested in winning field hockey games. She was also intent on helping her girls win in the game of life. That was why it wasn't surprising when she showed up at the Sheriffs' house to offer support to Nicole even though she had never met her future player before.

She had picked a good day to stop by for a visit. It was the winter of Nicole's eighth grade year. A bunch of girls from the field hockey team also happened to be at the house, and Coach Anthony just became another one of the girls as they all talked and shared stories about school times, sports times, and boy times. From then on, Coach Anthony would stop by the house on occasion to see Nicole. They would talk a lot about Nicole's former involvement with sports. One time Coach Anthony, who was also the head high school softball coach, asked Nicole why she stopped playing softball.

"I was a pretty good pitcher, you know," Nicole started.

"I know," Coach Anthony said. "That's why I asked."

"Well there was a time when me and my friends were joining these travel softball teams. Then I started getting phone calls at night from different coaches who wanted me on their team. They called some of my friends too. They were pulling me in different directions and I didn't think it was right. So I just said I wasn't going to play for anybody. I haven't played softball on a team since."

Coach Anthony was impressed with her young friend's sense of righteousness. She too agreed that adults sometimes took the fun out of sports for so many young people.

Sometimes, Coach Anthony and Nicole would discuss Nicole's future sports plans. "I miss basketball a lot," Nicole said. "I definitely plan to play that again. And I'm a really good field hockey player. I hope some day I can play for you."

Coach Anthony encouraged that thought and told Nicole she looked forward to having her on the team when she got well.

During July going into Nicole's freshman year, Nicole and Coach Anthony's schedules were such that they didn't get to see or talk to each other at all. When Nicole came back from Florida and the Disney vacation, there was just one week to go until the Pennsylvania fall high school sports teams were allowed to practice. Nicole hadn't communicated her plans to Coach

Anthony that she wouldn't be able to play field hockey and that she was going out for tennis. But Coach Anthony knew. She knew everything that was going on with her players. Before the season officially kicked off and the hectic days of August practices and the season began, Coach Anthony decided to take a ride up the hill to see how her young friend was doing.

When Coach Anthony pulled up, she found Nicole hitting tennis balls against her garage door. Nicole was alone for the afternoon. Linda had gone shopping and Doug was at school. Coach Anthony eyed the racket in Nicole's hand. "That's a funny looking field hockey stick. I don't think it's legal," she chided Nicole.

"It's a new racquet my father bought me," Nicole said. "You know I can't go out for field hockey, don't you?"

Coach Anthony nodded. "Is your tennis game as good as your field hockey game?" she asked.

"I wish. But I've been practicing whenever I can. My dad even got a mini net for the driveway so we can practice. He's not crazy about me hitting balls against the garage door."

They were standing in the driveway with the early August sun beating down on them. Nicole was wearing shorts and a bathing suit top. The sweat glistened on her body. Coach Anthony took notice of just how thin she had become. Deb looked toward the house and asked, "Is anybody home?"

"No. Do you want to come in?"

"Sure. That's why I came over."

When they got inside, Nicole saw the message light beeping on the phone. She hit the button. "Nicole, are you there?" It was her father. Then she checked her cell phone and saw that her dad had called that number too. "He's gonna kill me," Nicole told Deb. "I left the phones inside."

Just then she heard his truck pull up and his door slam shut.

"Oh my God," Nicole whispered to Deb. "Don't tell him I was hitting tennis balls against the garage."

"Your secret's safe with me," Deb whispered back to her.

When Doug came in, he was relieved to see that Nicole was fine. "I was outside and left the phone inside," Nicole explained. "I'm sorry."

"It's okay, Sweet Pea," Doug said. Then he turned to Deb. "So, are you still trying to recruit her for field hockey?"

Coach Anthony laughed. "I guess tennis is better than cheerleading," she said.

After a while of small talk, Coach Anthony got up and said to Nicole, "Well, I've got to get going. But I just wanted to wish you luck with tennis. I'll be watching out for you. And if you ever need anything, you let me know. I'll stop by when I can, but it gets pretty crazy during the season."

Doug and Nicole walked her to the door. Doug expressed his gratitude for Coach Anthony's time. "I'm sorry she's not going to get the chance to play for you," he told Deb.

"I am too," she said. "Good luck."

Coach Anthony was true to her words to Nicole. On the first day of practices, the field hockey team was practicing near the tennis courts. While there was a lull in her schedule, Coach Anthony made her way over to the tennis coach. The coach was watching the girls as they completed a series of movement drills. Nicole finished last in her group.

"How's it going, Coach?" Coach Anthony started.

"Well, they're not the most talented bunch, but they do work hard."

"How's Nicole Sheriff doing?"

"She has some skills and she works hard, but she's not one of the top ten. I'm not sure she's going to make the cut," the coach replied.

"You're thinking about cutting her?" Deb was incredulous.

"Coach, she's not one of the best."

"You realize she's got cancer, right?"

"Yes, her father explained her condition to me?"

"Then why would you cut her?"

"Because I only carry the best ten players."

"Coach, Nicole Sheriff may not be one of your top ten players, but the other girls will learn a lot just being around her. She'll give you everything she's got. The other girls will learn about perseverance and determination from her."

"I'll think about it. I don't plan on making any decisions until Thursday."

Coach Anthony walked back to her practice shaking her head.

The practices knocked Nicole out each day. Sometimes she would have to sit off to the side because the combination of sun and heat was too much for a body still taking oral chemotherapy and fighting off cancer. This was what had originally concerned Northampton High School's athletic director Mike Schneider. When Doug had come to him to ask his permission for Nicole to be able to participate in a sport, Mike wondered if Nicole was healthy enough to endure the practices and the workouts.

"Look, Mike," Doug explained. "I'm not looking for her to get any playing time. I just want her to be a part of a team, to have some semblance of a healthy teenager's life. She's got a major battle ahead of her. The prognosis from the doctor's isn't too good. I want her to be able to do what makes her happy."

Mike had already anticipated Doug's request. By law, all athletes have to have a physical and be medically cleared to participate in athletics. Mike knew no doctor was going to give Nicole Sheriff a clean bill of health so she could play a sport. It was Mike's job to protect the school from being liable for any health related accidents involving its athletes. Ordinarily, he was leery of parents suing the school if something did happen to their child. But in this case, he knew he didn't have to worry about that with Doug and Linda Sheriff. Doug had even told Mike he would sign any waiver he would need to in order to let Nicole play. Mike contemplated Nicole's condition. He was hearing from medical people he knew that when Ewing sarcoma returns, the average survival time patients lived was less than a year. He declared Nicole eligible to participate on Northampton's sports teams.

There were some moments when Nicole would show flashes of just how athletic she had always been. One day the coach said to her, "Are you sure you haven't been playing this game a long time. You're good. Things just seem to come to you naturally." When Doug would ask Nicole at night how things went that day, Nicole told him how the coach had used her several times during the practices to demonstrate the proper technique of a shot she was trying to teach the team. She thought things were going really well. Doug and Linda were just happy that Nicole was staying active.

On Thursday Nicole immediately burst into tears when she walked through the door of her home. "What's wrong, Nicole?" Doug asked.

"I got cut, Dad. Me and two other girls didn't make the tennis team." She cried even harder now. She was angry, tired, frustrated, and slightly embarrassed all at once. "All I wanted was to be part of a team and she cut me. And I worked so hard too." She was hysterical now. Doug and Linda worked together to console her and comfort her.

When Nicole was clam, Doug picked up the phone and dialed Mike Schneider's number.

"Mike, this is Doug Sheriff calling. Look, I'm not calling you as a parent now. I'm calling you athletic director to athletic director. Are you aware that Nicole was cut from the tennis team today?"

There was dead silence on the other end for a full ten seconds. Doug thought he had been cut off. "Mike, are you still there?"

"I'm still here. I'm floored. I'm pissed off."

"Mike, she knew Nicole's situation. Why would a coach cut a kid like that?"

"Doug, I don't have a good explanation for you. I saw Nicole working out his week at practice while I was walking our new superintendent around. I pointed Nicole out to her and told her Nicole's story. I'll call you back."

After he hung up, Doug turned to Nicole and said, "I'll bet you're going to be getting a call from your coach within the hour."

Nicole turned to her father and said, "Dad, I don't want to be on that team now. If I can't make it on my own, I'm not going to be a part of it."

Mike did immediately call the tennis coach. When she answered her phone, Mike greeted her with a question: "Do you understand what you did today?"

"What are you talking about?" the coach asked.

"You cut Nicole Sheriff, a girl who you know is battling cancer!"

"Mike, she wasn't one of the best ten and you said yourself you wanted us to keep our numbers under control this year."

"In this case, you could have kept one more. You don't understand what you did," Mike pointed out. "This is more important than numbers and who's the best. You need to rectify this immediately."

As Doug had predicted, the phone rang a half hour later. Nicole picked it up. It was the coach. She apologized to Nicole and offered her an opportunity to continue being a member of the tennis team."

"Thanks, but no thanks," Nicole told her. "I'll find something else to do."

Nicole wasn't sure what that was yet, but she was positive she didn't want to play tennis anymore. She sat and sulked on the couch until Doug said he was taking her and her mother out to Paolo's, their favorite local restaurant.

After dinner, Nicole asked Doug if they could drive by the field hockey field. She knew they were practicing late that night and she thought it might do her good to stop by and watch her friends practice. As she and Doug approached the field, a few of her friends caught sight of her and started to race towards her. Nicole couldn't contain her tears. The events of the day just made her miss field hockey and her friends more than ever.

When coach Anthony saw the swirl of commotion she made her way over. She noticed the tears running down Nicole's face and moved past Nicole and over to Doug.

"Don't tell me she cut her," she said to Doug. Doug just nodded. "I just talked to her on Monday. She said she thought she was going to cut Nicole and I said to her 'Why would you want to cut someone with such spirit and passion?' I guess she didn't get it."

Coach Anthony walked over to Nicole. She put her arm on her friend and said, "You know what, Nicole? You were born to be a field hockey player. You weren't born to play tennis. You're a team player, not a singles player. Do you still want to be a part of this team?"

Nicole's eyes widened. She emphatically shook her head in the affirmative. "Well then, you're on the team. You can be my manager. You can run drills and keep the stats. How's that sound to you?"

"Thanks, Coach Anthony. That sounds great."

The girls cheered and hugged Nicole. Then they went back to practice. "Go home and get your stuff together. We have practice tomorrow at 6 PM sharp," Coach Anthony directed Nicole.

That night, Nicole put her bag together and filled it with shorts and shirts and socks. She taped her stick and cleaned off her cleats. In the morning, she would be ready to finally call herself a member of the Northampton High School field hockey team.

Nicole had to stop by the hospital in the morning for a series of tests to see if the cancer was progressing or regressing. When she was meeting with Dr. Monteleone she said to him, "Dr. Phil, guess what. I've decided that I'm playing field hockey again."

"No you're not," the doctor replied sternly.

"Oh yes I am," Nicole insisted.

"You're not allowed to play field hockey, Nicole. There can be some serious consequences if you get hit where the tumor is."

"I don't care. Look, Doctor Phil. You guys are saying my chances aren't good anyway. So I'm playing. What do I have to lose?"

Dr. Monteleone didn't have a response to that question, and so later that day, Nicole stepped onto the field hockey field for the first time in almost two years. During Nicole's first few days of practice, Deb had her time drills and write down notes she would give her regarding things the team still needed to work on. Then Nicole was allowed to shoot at the goalies while the rest of the team conducted drills. After a few more days, Nicole let Deb know that being a manager wasn't going to be good enough. She wanted to participate in drills and be considered a player.

Before Deb or Doug could allow Nicole to participate in drills, they needed to find something that would protect the area on her back where the tumor was. Coach Anthony had a former player who had once broken her back. Deb remembered that this girl, who was now in college, had a special back brace she had used to protect her back. She placed a call to the girl and explained Nicole's situation. The girl was more than glad to let Nicole use the brace. She got it to Deb in just a few days. Nicole tried to practice with it on, but it was tight and restrictive and caused Nicole to sweat profusely. Nicole would then have to take it off after just a short period of time.

Doug, however, had come across something he thought would better serve their purpose. It was a motor cross belt designed to protect a rider's kidneys. When he put it on Nicole, it fit perfectly over the spot that needed to be protected. Nicole could now participate in drills!

On the day when uniform numbers were being assigned, Nicole went up to Coach Anthony and said, "I want number 34. That's always been my number. It's good luck."

But Coach Anthony, who was very much aware of Nicole's affinity for number 34, turned to her and said, "Nicole, you're just a freshmen. You get last picks. If it's here you can have it, but

I can't guarantee it. Get in the back of the line with the rest of the freshmen."

The seniors made their way into the gym, where the kilts and tops were laid out in piles. Coach Anthony sat behind a table and did a final check out of the uniforms the girls chose. When no one was looking, Deb scooped up jersey number 34 and sat on it while the upperclassmen chose their numbers.

When Nicole came in with the rest of the freshmen, she sifted through every pile looking for her number. Then she made her way over to Coach Anthony. "Coach, I don't see number 34," she said. "Was it taken?"

"Well maybe it's not here," Coach Anthony responded. "Why don't you try number 33 or number 4 or number 3?" Nicole shook her head. "How about number 7? That's 3 plus 4." Nicole shook her head again.

As the other freshmen were looking for anything decent among the uniforms that remained, Coach Anthony called Nicole back over to the table. Then she got up and revealed that number 34 had been stashed away under her butt all morning long.

"You're so mean," Nicole told her and glared at her with a look that was intended to be mean but couldn't disguise a smile. "Thanks, coach," she finally said.

———

Some days, Nicole was able to participate in most of the drills at practice. Other days, when she wasn't feeling well, she would sit with Deb or shadow her as she conducted drills. Deb started to talk to Nicole as if she were a coach. She even told her, "If you can't play it, you can at least coach it."

This was a job Nicole took very seriously. She thought nothing of yelling at girls, even seniors, who weren't trying hard in the drills. There were times when the medication Nicole was on caused her to be quite nasty. Her temperament was such that she would scream and curse at the girls for messing up in a drill. Most girls accepted Nicole's criticism and mood swings, but a few girls began to resent Nicole and her attitude.

One girl in particular took strong offense to what she called "Nicole's antics." She began to complain about Nicole to the other members on the team. "I'm sick of her screaming and her superior attitude," she would say. "Who does she think she is?"

It didn't take long for Nicole to hear the talk. The girl would say things just loud enough for Nicole but not Coach Anthony to hear. At first Nicole ignored it. She continued in her role as player - coach. Then one day Nicole overheard the girl talking to other teammates about her. "It's easy to scream at people for screwing up if you're not on the field," the girl explained. Some of the other girls agreed. Then this girl announced for all to hear: "Cancer or no cancer, Nicole Sheriff is a stuck up, spoiled bitch who gets preferential treatment, and I'm tired of it." The words were harsh and hurtful and they tore at Nicole's heart.

Nicole stormed out of the locker room, her closest friends right on her heels. She was angry, frustrated, and hurt by the comments. Outside in the parking lot, she broke down in a way her friends had never seen her do. Kera immediately pulled out her cell phone and called Linda. She explained to Linda what had transpired. "Some of the girls were really being nasty. I think you need to come down here and pick her up," Kera said. Linda was in the car a few seconds after she hung up.

In the car on the way home, Nicole broke down again and

cried. "She's saying such mean, hurtful stuff about me. Maybe everyone thinks that way about me. I don't want to go back there, Mom. I'm quitting," Nicole told Linda.

Not long after they were in the house, assistant coach Julie Marcks showed up at the door. "The girls said you left really upset and I just want to know what's going on," Coach Marcks said.

Nicole recapped the events for Coach Marcks. By the time Nicole got to the end of her story, she was crying again. Then she emphatically added, "I'm quitting field hockey, Coach Marcks. I'm not going back to that team."

Coach Marcks tried to console Nicole and dissuaded her from her thoughts about quitting. Coach Marcks then called Coach Anthony to inform her of the circumstances happening between the girls. Coach Anthony told Coach Marcks to tell Nicole she couldn't quit and that she would handle the situation at tomorrow's practice. Coach Marcks also assured Linda that what was going on was typical teenage behavior. It had nothing to do with Nicole's cancer. It was just girls being girls. "It happens all the time on teams for one reason or another. It's a good life lesson for Nicole."

The next day, Coach Anthony pulled the girl who was bad mouthing Nicole aside before practice. Coach Anthony told the girl, "I have been made aware of what you have been saying about Nicole. Do you understand that Nicole Sheriff is fighting for her life? You're being intolerant of a girl who is on medication, is fighting a disease, and who may not have long to live. I think you need to learn to be more tolerant of others and aware of their situations. Do you understand?" The girl nodded yes and Coach Anthony started to walk away. Then she abruptly turned around. "And let me be perfectly clear. If it comes down to me having to decide who stays on the team, you or Nicole, guess who's going? You are. So find a way to work it out."

The issue never surfaced again the rest of the season.

———

Right before the game season started Nicole approached Coach Anthony after practice and handed her coach a brochure Nicole had made up. "Coach, I have this idea, but I'm going to need your help. My parents and I have started a foundation called Angel 34. I want to raise money to help other people with cancer. One of the things I really want to do is to get an ICEE Machine for the children at Lehigh Valley Hospital."

"An ICEE Machine?" Coach asked.

"Yeah. After chemo and radiation, it's so hard for cancer patients to keep any food down. Plus you develop all these open sores in your mouth that hurt like anything. My father used to bring me ICEEs because that was the only thing I could keep down so I wouldn't dehydrate. Plus, the cold ice felt really good on the mouth sores. I want to raise enough money so I can buy an ICEE machine that will provide ICEEs for all the kids there. It'll help them feel a little better."

"That's really great on your part, Nicole," Coach Anthony told her. "Now what do you want me to do?"

"I thought that maybe before each game you could give a copy of this brochure to the other coaches and see if the other field hockey teams want to help me raise the money. It's a good cause."

Coach Anthony was amazed again at this girl's ability to think of others while she was suffering at the same time. When she would visit Nicole, Nicole would always tell her about the other kids at the hospitals who were a lot worse off. Nicole was always perplexed by the fact that some kids didn't have parents who were always there for them. She was constantly sending Doug and Linda out to buy little gifts for the other kids. The idea to raise money for an ICEE machine was just another example of Nicole's genuine concern for others.

Of course Coach Anthony agreed to help Nicole. And so before each varsity game, Coach Anthony would go over to the opposing coach and hand out a brochure and explain Nicole's illness and her fund raising idea. Most teams would then go back to their schools and raise money and send the money in to the Angel 34 Foundation.

Despite her illness, Nicole still showed a propensity for helping others in need. It was no different than her elementary school days when she would bring kids who were having bad days in to see Sue Carlson.

One day before a game, Coach Anthony saw that Nicole was visibly upset. Usually she warmed up the goalies and then would sit with Deb during the games shouting out encouragement to her teammates. Deb would point out how a player was out of position or didn't use proper technique. She was grooming Nicole to become a coach. But this day, Nicole didn't warm up the goalie. Instead, Deb came over to her as she was sitting on the bench. Tears rolling down Nicole's face. "What's wrong, Nicole?" Coach Anthony asked.

"I can't feel my legs. They're starting to get really numb. I can't feel them, Coach."

"Okay, stay calm, Nicole. I'll call your mom on my cell and tell her to come pick you up." She immediately called Linda and described Nicole's symptoms. Linda said she would be right there. "Your mom's on her way," she assured Nicole. Coach Anthony had to get back to preparing her team for the game but she didn't want to leave Nicole alone. She called over a team member who wasn't dressed for the game that day because she was recovering from an eating disorder. She asked the girl if she would sit with Nicole. The girl agreed to.

A little while later when Coach Anthony looked over to check on Nicole, she noticed that Nicole was doing most of the talking to the senior. Nicole was explaining to the girl, who was suffering from bulimia, how hard it was for her to keep her weight up with her illness. She told her all about how sick she had gotten when she was on chemo.

When Linda came, Coach Anthony helped get Nicole into Linda's car. "Coach Anthony," Nicole started before her mother pulled away. "I don't understand it. I try so hard to eat and she doesn't want to eat. I tried to tell her to eat and how she can make herself healthy. I just don't get it."

"It's alright, Nicole. I'm sure you gave her something to think about. Now go take care of yourself," Coach Anthony said. *Typical Nicole,* Coach Anthony thought to herself as she was heading toward the game. *Always thinking of other people before herself.*

In October, Nicole had to go for an MRI. The doctors wanted to keep a close watch on the progression of the tumor. The Sheriffs all gathered in Dr. Monteleone's office the next day to hear his interpretation of what the MRI revealed. He clipped the slides into their holders on the lighted reader. Then he turned to the family with a look of perplexity. "I don't believe these images myself," he started. "But take a look. The tumor's gone. It's disappeared. We've never had a response like this to this medicine. It was mainly a palliative type of chemo, but it made the tumor disappear."

Nicole gazed up at the image of her spine and organs and shifted her eyes between the before and after images. The blotch that appeared on her spine in the first slide was clearly not there in the second slide.

"I'm just amazed at the response. I hope it's a sign of good things to come," Dr. Monteleone said.

Nicole smiled as she looked from the images to her mother, and father, and doctor. They were all staring and nodding at the slides. "I told you, Doc. Don't stop believing in me," Nicole ordered them. "Don't ever stop."

———

As the field hockey season was winding down, Coach Anthony made the decision that Nicole Sheriff was going to get in a varsity game this season. She went to Mike Schneider one day and said, "Mike, I've got to get Nicole Sheriff in a game. She's been through so much this season that she deserves to see the field at least once. I don't care what has to be done, but she's playing." Mike knew there was no sense in arguing with Coach Anthony on this one, and so he gave his approval.

On the day of the Whitehall game, Coach Anthony made a point to find Nicole during the morning. "Do you have all of your equipment for field hockey?" Deb asked Nicole when she saw her.

"No, I don't have my cleats or my back pad. We have a game today, Coach. I don't need that stuff," Nicole replied.

"You're going to need it today," Coach Anthony told her. "I'm getting you in to today's game." Deb couldn't hold back a laugh when she saw the look of elation on Nicole's face.

Nicole immediately went and called Doug and told him the news. "What do you think, Dad? Can I play?" Nicole asked.

"Yeah. Go for it!" Doug said. "Call Mom and ask her to bring you your cleats."

When Nicole called her mother and announced that Coach Anthony planned to use her in the game that day, Linda immediately voiced her opposition to the idea. "There's no way you can play, Nicole. You can get hurt."

"I already called Daddy and he said I could," Nicole said.

Linda hung up with Nicole and called Doug. "Doug, there is no way can she play in that game."

"Linda, she already called me and I already said yes. I can't go back now. Besides, I think it will be a great experience."

Linda knew she had been trumped by her daughter who was smart enough to call her daddy first and get his blessing to play. Once she and her daddy had made an agreement, mommy had no chance to undo it. Linda left work to swing by the house so she could pick up Nicole's cleats and back pad.

Before the game, Coach Anthony had Nicole's brochure in her hand when she went over and spoke with the Whitehall coach. As she did before every game, she explained that she had a player who was suffering from Ewing sarcoma and that despite her own troubles, this girl was trying to raise money to purchase an ICEE machine so the children who still had to undergo chemo therapy and radiation could find relief in the frozen drinks. The Whitehall coach took the brochure and said she would present the information to her team.

Coach Anthony shook the coach's hand and turned to head back to her team. But then she abruptly turned around to the Whitehall coach who was getting ready to get back to her team. "Coach," Deb Anthony started. She pointed to the brochure that was still in the coach's hand. "That girl's name is Nicole, as you can see on the brochure. I'm going to get her in sometime today. She hasn't played a minute all season because of the cancer and how frail her body is, but I'm getting her in today."

The other coach seemed to understand the enormity of the action. "I'll be watching for her, Coach." They smiled at each other in understanding and turned back to their teams.

Midway through the second half, Coach Anthony turned to Nicole and said, "You better loosen up. You're going in pretty soon."

When Doug and Linda saw Nicole get up to warm up, they couldn't say another word to each other. Doug felt a lump build up in his throat and he didn't try to stop the tears flowing down his cheeks. Ever since the doctors had told Nicole she wouldn't be able to play sports, Doug wasn't sure he was ever going to get a chance to see Nicole perform again. But today, his little girl was going to be back in action on the field hockey field. This was the way it was always supposed to be.

At halftime, Coach Anthony had gone up to Nicole's friend Krista and asked, "Krista, would you mind if I take you out sometime this half so Nicole can play?"

"That'll be awesome, Coach. I won't mind at all," Krista replied.

As the time was approaching for Nicole to enter the game, she turned to her coach and nervously said, "Coach, I don't know if I can do this. I don't know if I'm ready for this."

Coach Anthony had seen hesitancy in Nicole sometimes when she was involved in team drills. In one of their personal discussions,

Nicole admitted to her she was scarred a bit about what could happen. The doctors said if she were hit on the spine where the tumor was located she could be paralyzed. It was understandable. And so was Nicole's doubt about entering this game.

But Coach Anthony showed faith in Nicole and showered her with encouragement. "Nonsense, Nicole," she started. "You're an athlete and you're going to play in this game." She wasn't a consoling friend anymore, but an encouraging coach. "You're just as capable as anyone on this field. So when you go out there, you play hard. It will all come right back to you."

Coach called a time out. As the team was huddled around her, Coach Anthony looked at Krista. "Krista, you're out for now." Then she looked at Nicole. "Sheriff, you're in. Go to left back."

When her teammates heard the order they started screaming and cheering. The girls knocked sticks with her for good luck. When the ref blew the whistle, Nicole and her teammates ran onto the field and into their positions. The Northampton parents began to take notice of Nicole out on the field. The parents who rimmed the perimeter of the field broke out into applause. Somehow, word had even spread to the Whitehall parents and they were clapping in admiration as well. Her teammates who weren't in the game were standing on the edge of the field clapping and calling out Nicole's name.

Nicole took her position amid this uproar. The perpetual smile masked her nerves. She refused to get caught up in the commotion of all these people standing and clapping and rooting for her. She quickly gazed at her parents and could see the tears streaming down both of their faces. She turned away from them to concentrate on the ball, which was coming her way. She didn't hesitate to get her stick on the ball and had some successful hits. At each hit, her teammates roared.

For ten minutes, the Sheriffs watched their daughter as she played a game she loved. For ten minutes, she wasn't a sick girl battling a tempest inside her. It was more than Doug or Linda had hoped for when Coach Anthony had taken her under her wings when she was cut from the tennis team.

The outcome of the game didn't matter that day. It was a triumph for all of the Northampton girls because they were part of the biggest success story of their season.

Doug found out that the disease couldn't take away his daughter's competitive spirit and drive. That night at home, after the emotions of the day had faded into the darkness of the autumn sky, Nicole turned to her father and admitted, "You know, I wasn't exactly pleased with the way I played today. A couple of girls ran right by me and I let some girls dribble around me."

"Nicole, you did awesome."

"You know I wasn't even playing my position. I'm a mid, not a left back."

"Nicole, you were terrific," Doug stated.

"Next time, I hope I play mid," she said.

Chapter Nine

Throughout the fall, the one thing that was sure to put a smile on Nicole's face was the sight of Ben. Their relationship since seventh grade had fluctuated in its intensity day by day and week by week. Ever since they attended the 8th grade Farewell Dance together, they were more or less boyfriend and girlfriend, though neither acknowledged that officially. From the time Nicole returned to school and into the summer before ninth grade, they would frequently hang out with each other in the school hallways, at the community pool, and at athletic events. They would IM each other and Nicole would sometimes have her friends call him just to see if he liked her.

Right before the start of ninth grade, Doug noticed that they were getting more serious with each other. He and Nicole always had an open and direct line of communication with each other. It was Doug who was there for Nicole in the summer before seventh grade when she got her first period. So now, as he found Ben calling more often and stopping by the house more than occasionally, he questioned his daughter about her relationship with this boy.

"Do you consider him your boy friend exclusively?" Doug asked her.

"Yes, Daddy," Nicole answered.

"Do you think he considers you his girlfriend exclusively?" Doug asked Nicole.

"Yes, Daddy. We want to be able to go on dates together. Alone," she admitted.

"I don't have a problem with that," Doug explained. "But before you really start dating, I'd like to meet his parents. I think it's important that I know what kind of household he comes from."

"That's fine with me," she said. "They're the nicest people."

Nicole was right in her judgment of them. The next time she saw Ben, she explained what her father wanted. The next night after that, Ben's mother pulled up in front of the Sheriff's house in her car while Doug was working in the front yard. Linda, Ben's mother and Doug talked for over an hour. The following night, Ben's father drove to the house and rang the front door bell. When Doug opened it, Ben's father introduced himself. Doug greeted him warmly and the two of them discussed how their children's relationship was evolving.

Soon Doug was reciting the history of Nicole's disease and detailing the hardships she had encountered throughout her battle. When he got to her present condition, he choked up a little and said, "The prognosis doesn't put the odds in her favor, but she's a battler and has every intention of defeating this thing." When Doug was finished, all Ben's father could do was shake his head. Doug allowed him time to take it all in and to attempt to comprehend the last two years of Nicole's life. Finally Doug offered, "So that's why I told Nicole I needed to meet you. I wanted to let you know all about her condition before they started dating."

"I respect that," Ben's father stated. "If that were my daughter, I'd do the same thing."

So when school began, Nicole and Ben were officially going out with each other. He would greet her at the flagpole each morning before school and slip his arm around her in an attempt to provide her warmth against the chill she often felt. They would go out to eat with each other's families and hang out at each other's houses. Ben was a goalie on the freshmen soccer team. When the varsity was playing a night game, he and Nicole would walk to the stadium and sit and watch the games together.

One night Doug had to drive Ben home after he had been at the house hanging out with Nicole. Nicole and Ben sat in the back seat of Doug's truck. Doug was alone in the front. He constantly glanced in the rearview mirror trying to figure out what was making Nicole laugh and giggle the way she was. When they got to Ben's house, Nicole walked him to the door. Under Doug's sentinel glare, they quickly hugged and Nicole ran back to the car, slipping in the front seat beside her father.

As Doug pulled away he asked, "What was so funny?"

"What do you mean?"

"You were carrying on the whole way to his house with that silly laugh. What was so funny?"

"He kept asking me if it would be all right if we hugged when we got to his house. It just made me laugh. I thought he was so funny."

Real funny, Doug thought to himself.

In October, after she had gotten into the field hockey game against Whitehall, the Northampton Booster Club honored Nicole. They invited her along with Doug and Linda to one of their games and presented her with a special courage award. It was just another warm gesture by the community. Nicole's struggle with Ewing sarcoma was well known throughout the town. But more importantly, so was her attitude and spirit. Everyone admired how Nicole and her family just tried to live life as normally as possible. Her appearance in the field hockey game was a testament to her will power and drive. It was for this, that the booster club wanted to recognize her.

What had also exceeded Nicole's expectations was her fundraising effort to raise money for the ICEE machine. What had started out as a whimsical idea to put a machine in the same children's ward where she had spent so many hours had turned into a full-fledged campaign. Nicole was hoping to raise 3,000 dollars to use as a down payment on a machine. But the field hockey teams from the surrounding communities really embraced the idea and continually sent money to Nicole throughout the season. In all, Nicole collected over 15,000 dollars.

Nicole had priced new ICEE machines at around 7,000 dollars. She was excited that she would actually be able to purchase two new machines. Then the local ICEE Company representative got wind of what Nicole was undertaking. He offered to get the machines for her at a much lower price; plus, he would provide a one-year maintenance plan at no cost. By the end of the field hockey season, Nicole was ecstatic at the fact that with the money collected from the other teams, she would eventually be able to purchase three machines.

With the success of the fundraiser, Nicole really began to think about how needy so many people were. She couldn't understand how when she was in the hospital, there were children there whose parents didn't stay with them or even visit them. She was always sending Doug or Linda out to purchase stuffed animals for the lonely children. She also knew of some children who weren't getting all of the medical help they needed because their parents didn't have insurance. "Maybe we should create an insurance fund just for children with medical needs," she told her father one day. This kind of thinking was the impetus behind the Sheriffs creating the Angel 34 Foundation. They knew they were fortunate in having medical insurance and in receiving the best medical treatment available. They knew they were fortunate in that they had family and friends to help them through this crisis. But they also knew so many others weren't as fortunate.

Nicole never saw herself as needy. But she had always had a great desire to help others in need. She envisioned a world where those who were in need of help would always be able to get it. With this vision in mind, she began to work with her parents to develop a foundation whose mission it would be to provide ICEE machines for more hospitals, money for families who had a child undergoing chemotherapy or radiation treatments, money for students who were going into the medical field, and money for continued research to find a cure for cancer. She decided to call this the Angel 34 Foundation. The number 34 represented Nicole. She hoped to always be an angel to those who were in need. Doug and Linda thought it was the perfect name. They would do the legal work to have the foundation recognized as an official charity organization.

The Northampton High School gymnasium was packed with screaming students who were there to show their support for the football team as it prepared for its big Thanksgiving Day game against archrival Catasauqua the next day. The cheerleaders danced and tumbled to the thunderous sounds of the band. The students were clapping and stomping their feet in rhythm on the wooden bleachers. As the music ended to yet another cascade of screams and cheers, the principal made his way to center court. "What a great show of support for our football team today," she started. "Now I'd like to take a moment to recognize the achievements of one among you who has been busy doing great things to help other people." The gymnasium grew eerily silent as the principal went on. "This is a young lady who is waging her own battle with Ewing sarcoma, a form of bone cancer. During this past field hockey season, she, along with the help of Coach Anthony and her teammates raised over 15,000 dollars to help others who are also suffering from the ravages of cancer. I think you all know her story. Today, I'd like to formally recognize her for her efforts. Nicole Sheriff, please come on out here."

Everyone did know her story. And during her first few steps towards center court, no one in the audience made a sound. Then one of her friends yelled out, "Yeah, Nicole." This was followed by other calls. Then some students started clapping to show their appreciation of Nicole's efforts and situation. The clapping moved like a wave throughout the crowd until it was thunderous. Her friends rose to their feet, and by the time Nicole reached the principal, she was in tears as the whole student body was on its feet roaring for Nicole. The principal shook her hand and then raised it and led Nicole to look at both sets of bleachers filled with her admirers.

The band began to play and the cheerleaders started to dance again as the pep rally was refocused back onto the upcoming football game.

Afterwards, many older boys who were members of various athletic teams kept coming up to Nicole to praise her and wish her good luck. Nicole basked in their attention. Ben jealously disappeared into the crowd.

———

One day in early December, Nicole became extremely lethargic. As soon as Linda saw her, she knew she needed to get Nicole to a hospital. The doctors ran a series of tests and screenings on Nicole in an attempt to assess the disease's progress. The MRI's revealed that the tumor was back and the blood test indicated that the cancer wasn't abating.

Exhausted from a stressful day, Nicole smiled when she saw Ben and his father at her hospital room door. "How's it going?" Ben asked.

"I've had better days," Nicole responded.

Doug and Ben's father engaged in small talk as Linda, Nicole and Ben sat on the bed talking and watching TV. Suddenly, all color disappeared from Nicole. She looked gaunt and ghostly. A nurse suddenly appeared at Nicole's side and quickly took Nicole's blood pressure and pulse. She studied Nicole's chart. "Her blood counts are probably bottoming out," the nurse surmised. She called for assistance and for an IV bag. "Immediately," she stressed into the call box.

Another nurse turned Nicole's hand palm up and began feeling up and down Nicole's arm. She injected the needle but knew immediately she hadn't hit a vain. She asked another nurse to come help her. "I can't find a vein," she told the other nurse.

The nurses kept searching up and down Nicole's arm for a place to insert the IV needle.

Doug turned to Ben. "You can go now if you want to Ben. I don't know what's going to happen. You don't need to see this if you don't want to."

"I'll stay with her," Ben said. Ben looked at his own father who had an, "Are you sure you're up for this?" look on his face. Ben nodded several times. Then he moved towards Nicole and held her hand. He stared at the frail hand and looked carefully up at Nicole. She weighed just 104 pounds now and was wearing no wig. Still, he held her hand as the nurses scurried around them.

"Shut the light," one nurse ordered.

Immediately, the room light was shut, the door was closed, and a nurse was holding a light bulb under Nicole's hand. The light could be seen through her slender hand and wrist. More importantly, the nurses followed the shadowy lines up her slim arm and were able to detect the spot where they could be sure to hit a vein. Within seconds the IV was draining into Nicole and nurses were withdrawing from the room. When the lights were turned back on, Ben was still holding Nicole's hand.

A few days later, Linda and Nicole were in their kitchen baking cookies for the Christmas season. Nicole was mixing baking ingredients and talking to Ben on the phone at the same time. After a while, Ben suggested that they get off the phone and IM each other. Nicole was agreeable to his suggestion and hung up the phone. "I'll be right back, Mom," Nicole said. "Ben wants to IM instead of talk." Linda just nodded and continued with her preparations. Nicole went upstairs to use the computer.

About a half hour later, Doug was walking past Nicole's room when he heard her crying. He walked into the room and found Nicole in tears. Torn up photos of Ben littered the floor. "How could he do this to me?" Nicole was shouting. "How could he do this to me?"

"What happened, Nicole?" Doug asked, having already deduced what had just taken place.

"He broke up with me, Dad," Nicole cried out. She started to repeatedly smash a throw pillow onto the couch. Doug called for Linda to come upstairs immediately. As soon as Linda entered the room, Nicole broke down in her mother's arms.

"He asked me to IM him instead of talking to him on the phone and then he broke up with me. He didn't even have the nerve to do it in person. He said he still cared for me and everything but that he just didn't want to go out with anyone at this point in his life. He thought we were getting too serious and he needed more room. It was like a whole speech he had prepared. He didn't even have the nerve to tell me to my face!"

Linda could only hold her and rock her and rub her back. "This happens sometimes with boys, Nicole," she whispered, but she knew it was no comfort.

"I hate him," Nicole said. "I really hate him for hurting me like this. And I hate having cancer. Because you know that's what did it. That's what drove him away."

Linda couldn't dispute Nicole's interpretation. "I'm sure he's afraid, honey. It's a lot for a 15-year-old boy to deal with. He's probably just afraid and unsure."

Linda could only hold her daughter and be there for her as she was every day of her life.

⸺

The day after Thanksgiving, Nicole packed her gym bag and announced to her parents, "I'm going out for basketball. I don't care what the doctors say. I'm playing."

The new high school coach, Craig Mogel, just happened to

be the guy who had coached Nicole's middle school team. Nicole had enjoyed playing for him then and was thrilled that he had been offered the varsity head girls basketball coaching job. She had already spoken to him about her intentions, and since the precedent was set by Nicole's participating in field hockey, Coach Mogel was more than welcoming of Nicole in his program.

In the early December practices, Nicole was allowed to do some one on one drills and some individual skills work, but she was not allowed to participate in full team scrimmages. Not that she was up for that anyway. Each day, she felt more fatigued and participated less and less in the practices. The last time she had gone to visit Dr. Stern, the news she received wasn't so good. The chemotherapy she was currently taking was not having an impact on the cancer's progress. The doctors were reaching now to try and find the right combination of drugs that would be able to stymie the advance of the cancer. This explained Nicole's lack of energy and her inability to compete. The cancer was taking from her all the natural speed, strength and fluidity which had allowed her to be such a gifted athlete throughout her elementary years.

Then one night when Doug was home, the phone rang. It was Coach Mogel. "Doug, I need to act in Nicole's best interests," he started. "A number of girls on the team are sick and it seems to be passing from one girl to the next. I'm fearful that Nicole could catch something that could knock her out. I don't think she should continue to be around the team as closely as she has been."

Doug understood and appreciated Coach Mogel's concerns. Recently, Nicole had to stay home a number of times from school because she felt weak. Doug knew her resistance to infections was almost nonexistent. It was almost getting to the point where sending her to school could be detrimental to her health. He thanked Coach Mogel and agreed that Nicole shouldn't be with the team right now. "Maybe when everyone's in good health Nicole could return," Doug said, but he only half believed that himself. Coach Mogel obligingly agreed.

~~~

Nicole solemnly accepted the news regarding her basketball status. She had a feeling this was coming. Besides, she was having trouble just making it to school now, and when she was there, she often had to come home. Doug and Sue Carlson agreed that Sue would be needed more often now to help Nicole keep up with her studies.

December was a difficult month for Nicole. She felt everything slipping away from her. She was having trouble attending school, she couldn't be on the basketball team, she no longer had a boyfriend, and she didn't get to see her friends much. Sue Carlson sensed all of this as she began to spend more and more time with Nicole, tutoring her and, more importantly, counseling her.

When Sue would come to the house, she would always bring two things: schoolwork and Lucy, her therapy poodle. The first time Sue had ever entered the Sheriff house as Nicole's homebound instructor, she had her apricot miniature poodle with her. Lucy was just a rambunctious pup then, but she and Nicole immediately bonded. Lucy was a good distraction for Nicole. She offered Nicole an outlet for her feelings. At first Lucy would constantly fidget in Nicole's arms. But as the two got to know each other more, Lucy settled down and became more sedate. When Nicole would grow tired of working on her studies, she would say, "I think Lucy needs a treat."

Most times, Sue would take this as a cue. She would then

suggest that they take a break from the schoolwork. It was during these downtimes when Nicole and Sue would really talk. Lucy would settle in on Nicole's lap and Nicole would pet her as they covered a great array of topics ranging from school issues, to friend issues, to cancer issues, and always back to boy issues. Sometimes Linda would be there with them, but Nicole always opened up more when her parents weren't around. As much as she loved them and needed them, she also worried about how her illness was affecting them. During the spring when her cancer went into remission, Nicole was informed that because of all the chemotherapy and radiation that had been introduced into her body, she would probably never be able to have a child. While it upset her for herself, she revealed to Susan that she was even more upset for her parents. "They'll never have grandchildren," Nicole lamented.

As always, Susan directed Nicole to understand her circumstance and to figure out an appropriate response to it. "Some things are out of your control," she would tell Nicole. Then she would ask, "So what can you control?" Regarding Nicole not being able to have children, Nicole and Susan explored other possibilities that could make Nicole a mother. They talked about adoption. "Just because you don't give birth to a baby doesn't mean you can't be a mother," Sue said. "Adopting a child would be like rescuing it from hardship. How would you like that?"

"That would be pretty cool," Nicole responded.

Susan always had a way of empowering Nicole to grasp and direct whatever she could. "How can you make lemonade out of lemons?" she would always ask Nicole.

As the year was slipping away with each gray day of December, Nicole grew more fatigued and sullen. She resisted doing the schoolwork Susan brought with her each day into the house. Doug took notice that they seemed to be talking more than they were working. "I don't think you're doing nearly enough math," he told Sue.

Susan responded, "You're right. I'm not." But she had made a decision that as Nicole's physical and mental health continued to slide, she was not going to make school a stress in Nicole's life. Nicole hated math and Susan wasn't about to force her to do something she hated. There were other more important subjects that needed to be addressed.

One day Doug and Linda left the house while Susan was tutoring Nicole. As soon as her parents left, Nicole decided that Lucy needed a treat. Lucy sat in Nicole's lap and ate the little treats Nicole fed her. As she always did, Nicole teased Susan about the ownership of the poodle. "Lucy really should be my dog," she would say. "Why don't you just leave her here?"

"She's got to go home," Susan would say.

After a while, as Nicole continued to stroke Lucy's head, she revealed what was on her mind. "I don't think I'm going to win this battle," Nicole finally admitted. She looked at Susan. "What if I don't win? What if I don't survive?" The tears flowed freely down her cheeks. "

In the spring of Nicole's fifth grade year, Linda's mother was diagnosed with terminal cancer. It wasn't until the following October when Nicole grew tremendously distressed. "My grandmother might die," she had told Sue then.

"So what can you do to help make the situation better?" she asked her young counselee. "What do you control?"

They decided that Nicole could make her grandmother cards

that would express Nicole's feelings for her. They also decided that Nicole would be sure to tell her grandmother all the things that she wanted to tell her so she would have no regrets.

Now, as Nicole brought up her current battle, Susan looked at Nicole. "What can you control?"

"I don't know," Nicole said, resisting Susan's attempt to allow her to open up.

"Come on," Susan coaxed her. "I know you've thought about it."

Nicole took a deep breath. "I can control how I spend my time. I can make each moment count."

"Good," Susan told her. "How are you going to do that?"

"I'm going to make sure those ICEE machines get put into the hospitals. I want to help raise money for families who can't afford to pay for doctors and medicine."

"Those are great things," Susan said.

But then Nicole looked down and a forlorn look came across her face.

"What's wrong?" Susan asked.

"I'm afraid people will abandon me when I really need them."

"I'll be here the whole time with you," Susan promised.

"I can't talk about this with my parents, you know. I don't think my father can accept what's happening to me."

"You're right," Susan told her. "But that's something you can't control now. You're just going to have to give him a lot of time. It won't be easy."

Nicole nodded that she understood. She stroked Lucy who was sitting serenely in her lap. She heard her mother's car pull into the driveway. "It feels better to talk about it," Nicole admitted.

"We'll talk about it again," Susan assured her. "Like I said, I'll be here the whole time with you."

⁓

At his school, Doug was the organizer of an annual trip to New York City with a group of Northampton students. They would go in to see the Christmas show at Radio City Music Hall and then walk the streets to Rockefeller Center. Nicole accompanied him on every trip. "Are you up for it this year?" Doug asked Nicole as December was approaching.

"I wouldn't miss this for anything," Nicole replied.

Nicole had developed the ability to draw on a reserve bank of energy to get her through some arduous activities. On the day of the trip, she endured a two-hour bus ride into the city, the hour and a half Christmas Spectacular, and a walk up and down the streets surrounding Rockefeller Center. The excitement of New York at Christmas time raised her adrenalin and she went through the day wearing a mesmerizing glow. She smiled as she enjoyed looking at each of Macy's animated windows.

One of the traditions Nicole and Doug had created on this trip was that they always bought something unique from one of the street venders. Nicole enjoyed the bartering process with the people who sold their items. At one vendor's stand, Nicole became enamored with a white hat. She began to bargain with the vendor over its price. After a while, she realized it was futile to continue negotiations with the vendor who was unwilling to come down in price on the hat. Nicole told him he was asking too much and walked away.

As Nicole and Doug and some of his teachers and students continued to meander down the street, Doug noticed that Nicole had started crying.

"What's wrong, Sweet Pea?" he asked her.

"Nothing," she said, but she continued to cry.

"Is it because you didn't get to buy that hat?" Doug asked. But Nicole just shook her head no.

Dave Heinman was a friend of Doug's and a teacher at Doug's school who had accompanied him on this trip. He had witnessed Nicole's crying and went about to help her feel better. He secretively went back to the vendor, purchased the hat, and gave it to Nicole as a gift. She thanked him and settled down as the group made its way down the city street. When Doug thought enough time had passed for him to broach the subject again, he asked Nicole, "What happened back there? Was it because you didn't get the hat?"

Nicole shook her head emphatically. "It wasn't the hat," she said. "I just happened to see some homeless guy back there begging for money." She started to tear up again. "I don't understand why there has to be homeless people. How can people not have a home?"

Doug was incredulous. Here was his daughter, in a life and death battle with cancer, and she was crying over a homeless man. Even as her illness was gaining strength, she was still concerned with the welfare of other people. He couldn't help but to be awed by her compassion. He put his arm around her and they made their way towards the tree at Rockefeller Center. He began to choke up himself when he thought about her condition. *This might be the last time my daughter can accompany me on something like this*, he thought to himself. He couldn't imagine being here without her. He shook his head to wipe that thought from his mind. It entered his thoughts every now and then, more often lately he noticed, but he always shooed it away quickly. He couldn't allow thoughts like that to linger.

Fortunately, his thoughts were quickly diverted this time as they turned between two buildings and caught sight of the magnificent and grandiose tree. All their attention was drawn to its glory. As he had done on each prior trip, Doug made Nicole pose in front of the tree as he took her photograph. Through the camera's lens, he saw nothing but a child's grin, caught up in the magic of the Christmas season in New York City.

～

In January, the team of doctors met with Doug, Linda and Nicole after they had performed another battery of tests on Nicole. "We're sorry to report that we're making no progress against the advance of the disease," Dr. Stern said. "We've tried everything conceivable to stifle its progress, but we haven't had any success." She looked at Doug and Linda. "I'm sorry, but it's just a matter of time before the cancer wins."

"How much time are we talking about?" Doug wanted to know. He wasn't shocked by the prognosis. In the back of his mind, he knew things weren't going well. He just never allowed himself to create a timetable. "We have a trip set up to take Nicole to Cancun in April. Will she be able to go on that?" he asked.

"Don't wait for April," Dr. Stern advised. "Go as soon as you can. As the disease progresses, it's going to be debilitating to Nicole. The tumor on her spine continues to grow and I'm not sure how much longer it will be before it cripples her. Move that trip up and go as soon as you can."

～

Nicole was supposed to have made her confirmation when she was in eighth grade. Unfortunately, she was going through her stem cell transplants while her friends were attending religion classes that were intended to prepare them for the rite of confirmation in the Lutheran Church. Doug and Linda had raised Nicole in faith. From the time she was an infant, Doug said nighttime prayers with Nicole. During her first couple of years he said them over her. Then, once she was able, he said them with her. Her relationship with God was more advanced than most teenagers her age. She would write to God in her journals, sometimes asking for strength and good health, and other times acknowledging that what she was going through was only strengthening her faith in Him. That was why she got so mad one time when she and Doug went to church shortly after she had completed her time in isolation after her stem cell transplant. It just so happened that the confirmation class she was supposed to be in was in church to celebrate mass. Many of the teens weren't paying attention and showed very little reverence for Jesus. After watching the class for most of the mass, Nicole finally turned to Doug and said, "Some of those kids don't even believe. They don't care about confirmation. You'll never see them in church again. I don't need a class to say I love the Lord. I believe. That should be me up there getting ready to make my confirmation." From that moment on, Nicole had made up her mind that somehow, she was going to be confirmed. Whenever an opportunity presented itself, Nicole pressed her parents to do something that would allow her to be confirmed.

In late February, word was getting around town that Nicole's condition was worsening. One day, the Sheriff's Pastor Gary inquired about Nicole's health. He had been there with the family when they made their first trip to Philadelphia. And now he was aware that she was apparently losing the battle. Doug told the pastor about Nicole's desire to be confirmed. Pastor Gary was very much aware of how Nicole had been unable to complete the confirmation class because of her treatments. Yet he was a bit reluctant to confirm someone who had not gone through the full confirmation process. However, after several members of the Church Council let the pastor know they would allow Nicole special consideration so she could be confirmed, Pastor Gary agreed to allow it as well.

Within a week, a special ceremony during which Nicole would make her confirmation was scheduled and prepared. Over 175 people came to the church, including a group of girls in their basketball uniforms, to watch Nicole receive the sacrament of confirmation. The pastor laid his hands on her shoulders and she received the Holy Spirit. Right then and there her faith in God was made even stronger than it had been before. It was an important moment in her life. Over the next few months, she would lean on that faith and rely on her relationship with God to guide and comfort her.

Less than two weeks later, the plans were set for Nicole to go on her trip to Cancun. Doug had a severe phobia to flying. On each flight to and from Disney the summer before, he broke out in a full body sweat and was on the verge of hyperventilating. He had made the decision that he wouldn't join Nicole and Linda on this trip. He had his time with her in New York and at all of the Philadelphia sporting events they attended together. The time in Cancun would be Linda's.

Doug and Linda allowed Nicole to ask a friend to accompany her. Nicole chose Samantha. She and Sam had always had so much fun together and she would be perfect to keep her spirits up during the trip. Doug drove the three of them to Philadelphia where they all spent the night. The next day, Linda, Sam, and Nicole took off for Cancun.

It was a great trip. Nicole had a fantastic time with Sam and spent some special time with her mother. She sent post cards home to Doug each day. She bought him a marble chess piece and a necklace to go with the cross she had given him for Christmas. She also got to spend more time swimming with dolphins. Their beauty and their apparent ability to communicate with humans mesmerized her. As she waded in the water, she stroked one dolphin's back. As she closed her eyes and listened to the other dolphins making sounds as they played, she felt a calming peace come over her.

Doug had hired a limo to pick up the girls and Linda from the airport. As Nicole, Sam, and Linda were coming out of the gate, Nicole noticed a driver holding up a sign that said, "Sheriff." Nicole saw it and grew excited at the thought that her daddy had sent a limo to pick them up. But as she tried to show her mother that there was a man holding up a sign with their name on it, she stumbled and fell to the ground. The driver raced towards this young girl who had suddenly fallen before him. "Nicole, are you all right?" Linda asked as she bent over her. But all Nicole, could say was, "The sign. The sign."

"What sign?" Linda asked.

By this time the driver was standing over Nicole, trying to help her up. Nicole pointed to his sign and Linda now understood.

"You wouldn't be the Sheriffs now, would you?" the driver asked, and they all laughed.

When Doug saw Nicole as she got out of the limo in their driveway, he immediately noticed a difference in Nicole. Her face was fuller, her arms seemed thicker, and her shoulders were broader. "My God, child. What did they feed you down there?" Doug wanted to know. But he knew the change in her appearance was due to the steroids the doctors had started Nicole on in an attempt to help her keep up her strength.

Doug took Linda and Nicole out to dinner that night. Over their favorite Italian dishes at Paolo's, he listened to them tell stories about their vacation and all the things they did. He laughed as Linda told him about how Nicole met their limo driver at the airport that afternoon. "She was so excited when she saw his sign, she just fell down and was sprawled out on the airport floor," Linda said.

After dinner, Doug drove them all home. As they were getting out of the car, he noticed that Nicole was struggling to get up. Once she did rise, he noticed she was struggling to maintain her balance. He thought that she was just exhausted from a long day of traveling. He went to her. "Do you want me to carry you, Sweet Pea?" he asked. She shook her head no and started to make her way up the walk to the house. Suddenly, she just collapsed. Her legs gave out and refused to support her weight. Nicole went down in a heap. Doug rushed to her, picked her up, and carried her the rest of the way into the house.

A few days later, as Nicole was walking in the hospital parking lot on her way to have her blood counts checked, her legs gave out again and she suddenly, without warning, found herself on the parking lot pavement. After her exam, a doctor explained to the Sheriffs what was happening to Nicole. "The tumor in her back is getting bigger," she explained. "It's beginning to press against her nerve, which is causing that sudden loss of control. Chances are, it's going to continue to get worse."

The next day, Doug had planned to take Nicole to see a 76ers basketball game in Philadelphia. As they were getting ready to leave for the game, Doug turned to Nicole and said, "Why don't I get a handicap sign for the car. That way we can park close to the stadium entrance." As he was talking, Linda tried to catch his attention behind Nicole's back. She was motioning for him to not bring that subject up. She and Nicole had already had this conversation and Nicole made it very clear to Linda what she thought about the idea. But Linda's warning was not received. Doug continued on. "There's no reason for you to have to walk so far. I'll just get a handicap sign for the car."

"I don't need a handicap sign," Nicole screamed at him. "I'm not handicapped. There are a lot of people a lot worse off than I am. I don't need a sign!"

Doug didn't argue.

Chapter Ten

In January, Doug and Linda started talking about adding a sunroom onto the back of their house. It would be a bright and airy place where Nicole could spend her days. They didn't say it aloud, but both knew that soon, getting Nicole up and down the stairs would become an extremely difficult and dangerous task. Whenever they talked about the new room in front of Nicole, Doug tried to make it sound like the addition was for him. But as was always the case, Nicole couldn't be deceived.

"You're putting this room in for me, aren't you?" she asked Doug one day.

"Yeah," Doug admitted. He could never lie to Nicole. "We are. We want you to have a comfortable room down here too."

"Well if it's for me, I want to design it."

"Okay," her dad agreed.

Doug put in a call to Jim Hamm, a builder whom Doug wanted to hire to get the work done. "I'm really busy right now, Doug," Jim told him. But then Doug explained Nicole's situation and the purpose for the room. "Timing's really important now," Doug added. Jim was so affected by what Doug had told him that he immediately dropped everything he was doing on his other jobs and began working at the Sheriffs' house. The twelve by twelve room would be a step down off the kitchen at the back of the house. And so as winter wore on, Jim began to hammer out the frame of the room and Nicole busied herself scouring through catalogues and home decorating magazines in a quest to find just the right furniture and décor for her special place.

Her physical condition deteriorated with each passing day. It got to the point where Doug and Linda had to hire a hospice nurse to help them take care of Nicole. Her walking had become so unstable that whenever she had to go somewhere in public, she had to use a wheelchair. She hated the wheelchair though and much preferred being carried by her father, who was only too happy to acquiesce to his daughter's requests. One time when Doug was carrying her upstairs to bed, Nicole asked him, "Daddy, do you mind carrying me all over the place?"

After Doug gently let her down on her bed, he looked at her and said, "God made me strong for a reason, Sweet Pea. And this is it. That's what I'm here for."

Nicole beamed a smile at her father.

As more time passed, Nicole started having accidents at night. She just couldn't get to the bathroom quickly enough. One particular night, Doug was awakened by Linda's voice. "Doug, can you come in here?" she called to her husband. "Nicole has to go to the bathroom and she can't make it. She needs your help."

Doug came whisking into the room, but just as he got there, he watched helplessly as Nicole was standing at the base of the bed, wetting herself. As the warm urine seeped through her pajama bottoms, their eyes met. Nicole's were immediately filled with tears. "Daddy, I'm…"

"Don't say it," Doug scolded her. He pointed his finger at her for emphasis. "Don't you dare say it!"

"But…"

"You never have to apologize to me for anything. Never," he told her.

He and Linda helped clean Nicole up and get her back to bed.

After these accidents happened a few more times over the next two weeks, the hospice nurse brought over a port-a-potty and placed it next to Nicole's bed.

The bathroom accidents weren't the only messes Nicole would make in her bed. The medications she was now on caused her to have an unsatisfied appetite. Often before bed, Nicole would binge on cake and glasses of milk. One late night, Nicole had a big glass of milk, which she planned to finish in bed while she watched TV. But she unexpectantly dozed off and the glass of milk fell over and emptied into her bed. She awoke with a scream. Doug was in the room without delay. "What's the matter?" he asked. "I spilled my milk," Nicole answered.

Doug was tired. He surveyed the damage in silence and began to strip the sheets from the bed. Nicole mistook his tiredness for anger and set out to dissolve the situation. She remained silent as she watched her father work, but she stared at him constantly with puppy dog eyes. He would glare up at her and set back to work, cleaning up the spill and getting out new sheets. She dropped her chin down to her chest and stared up at him with her sad eye gaze, believing her father was very angry with her. All at once, Doug stood up straight and smiled at her and said, "So-you got milk?" imitating a popular milk commercial on TV. They both began to crack up uncontrollably. "Oh, Daddy," she said affectionately.

Towards the end of March, the Sheriffs had gotten word from Muhlenburg Hospital that the ICEE machine Nicole had raised money to purchase was going to be installed. Nicole beamed with pride and satisfaction that the children there would reap the benefits of the tasty and popular drink. Then word came that the ICEE machine they had ordered for Lehigh Valley Hospital, the hospital where she personally went through countless medical procedures, was also being delivered.

"What do think, Sweet Pea?" Doug asked her. "Do you want to have a dedication ceremony?"

"Yeah that would be cool."

"Will you be up for actually going there?"

"I'll find a way. Let's do it."

"What do you think would be a good day?"

"Well, let me check my calendar, I'm so busy these days," Nicole teased her dad. Then she declared, "Let's do it on April 14th, my birthday. That's a gift I can give to other kids."

It struck Doug that his daughter never stopped amazing him with her thoughtfulness and courage. He smiled and agreed that that was a great date and then went about making the plans for the dedication.

A few days later, Nicole was once again invited by the Philadelphia 76ers basketball organization to be their guest at a game. Only this time, not only was she going to be a guest, she was going to be honored for her industrious work raising money for the ICEE machines. Before the game, several players came over to Nicole to say hello. She got to see her favorite player, Kyle Korver, whom Nicole adored. She liked the way he played basketball, but she loved the way he looked. He autographed a ball for Nicole. Doug wanted to purchase a Kyle Korver jersey for Nicole in the clothing store there, but the store was all out of them. Doug was able to speak with a woman named Brea in their community relations department and explained how he couldn't find the Korver jersey and why he wanted it. Brea said, "Don't worry, Mr. Sheriff. We'll take care of that. I promise to send you one in the next few days."

Another player named Eric Snow came over to Nicole and Doug while they were watching warm-ups from courtside. Eric recognized Nicole from a time he had visited CHOP to help hand out Christmas presents. When it was Nicole's turn to receive a present, the woman helping Eric apologized and said they were all out of gifts for girls. Linda jumped in and said, "No you're not. You've got a basketball there. That would be a perfect gift for my daughter." Now on this special night for Nicole, Eric Snow went out of his way to congratulate Nicole and let her know he remembered her.

In between the first and second quarters, Doug was asked to wheel Nicole out to center court as the public address announcer explained what Nicole had accomplished in raising the money and starting her foundation. The announcer then proclaimed Nicole a Philadelphia 76ers Hometown Hero. As Nicole received a plaque from the 76ers public relations man, the crowd rose to its feet and gave her a standing ovation in recognition and appreciation of her efforts. Nicole's face glowed with delight as Doug wheeled her back to their seats.

A few days later, Nicole awoke to celebrate her 15th birthday. This was also the day of the ICEE machine dedication. Nicole was exceedingly uncomfortable getting into the car to go to the hospital. "Nicole, if you are too uncomfortable to go, you don't have to," Doug told her. But Nicole insisted on attending. Her legs had become so weak that she lost the ability to walk at all now. Doug carried her when he could, but other times now, she was forced to use a wheelchair. When Doug wheeled her into the pediatric unit, Nicole was shocked to see that so many of her friends from her field hockey team had come out to help her celebrate this event. Doug had invited the girls and Deb Anthony because without their assistance, the money never would have been raised.

Gary Pierzga was there as well. He and Nicole maintained their contact with each other primarily because of their love of the 76ers. Gary used this day to present Nicole with the Kyle Korver jersey the 76ers organization had promised they would send. Nicole's face lit up when Gary unveiled it.

Many of her friends were taken aback at Nicole's appearance. Some hadn't seen her in a few weeks or even months and were stunned at the effects the steroids had taken on Nicole's body. They remembered an athletic dynamo with a sleek yet powerful body. What appeared before them was a bloated girl with chubby cheeks and plump features. Nonetheless, they hid their reactions and rejoiced in this festive dedication.

One person who was overcome at Nicole's appearance was Keith Groller, the local reporter who had written several articles on Nicole the year before. When he had interviewed Nicole then, she was the embodiment of health and exuberance. After all, she had just gotten word that she was cancer free. And now he stared at her in the wheelchair from across the room, but he couldn't approach her. He couldn't believe it was the same girl.

It took him fifteen minutes to work up the nerve to approach

Nicole. Even then, he was unsure how he would handle himself. But he had a story to write and needed to interview the day's guest of honor.

"Congratulations, Nicole," he said.

"Hi, Mr. Groller," Nicole replied. "Thanks for coming."

"It's my honor," he told her. Then he said, "Isn't it great that all of these people are here to pay tribute to you?"

She shook her head no emphatically and set out to correct this reporter so he could get the story right. "It's not about me, Mr. Groller. It's never been about me. What's great is that the ICEE machine and other money raised will help kids who are suffering. I know what that's like."

Mr. Groller shook his head in wonder and admiration. Then he checked his notes to make sure he got Nicole's quote right and the ICEE story straight.

As the work on the sunroom progressed, Nicole's body continued to degenerate. The cancer continued its assault on her body. In late April, the effects on her body became more dramatic. After Nicole completed one of her late night binges of chocolate cake and milk, Doug was helping his daughter to get situated in her bed. "What time do you have to go to school tomorrow?" Nicole asked her father.

"I have to leave here about 6:30," Doug replied.

"Wake me up at 6:00. I'll have breakfast with you."

Doug happily agreed to do as she said. He was always so grateful that Nicole still cherished her time with him.

When he went into her room at 6:00 to wake her up, Nicole looked at him with a startled and scared look.

"Daddy, I can't move my legs," she said. She remained calm, but was clearly frightened. Tears began to roll down her face. "I can't even feel them."

Doug did some preliminary checks of his own. He pinched her toes and flicked her foot. She had no feeling. He was shocked at how rapidly her condition could change. Just a few hours ago when he tucked her in, she had full movement. And now here, in the early morning, he discovered his daughter paralyzed from the waist down. Linda called the doctor immediately to report Nicole's condition and to find out if she and Doug should bring her in. The doctor's response made it clear that this was expected and it was not an emergency. "This is what we told you would happen," the doctor said, "as the cancer progressively invades the spine."

Doug was happy for one thing: that he made Nicole go to Cancun when she did. This was the week for which they had originally booked the trip before Dr. Stern strongly suggested they go in January. She knew then what was going to happen to Nicole. Doug had resisted thinking that Nicole would get worse. He had always held out hope for recovery. But as he left the house that morning, he broke down and cried; he knew now that his daughter was dying.

Nicole started to develop shingles all over her back. The skin ailment caused extreme discomfort. One of the few remedies for it was heat. Heat seemed to relieve some of the symptoms. Nicole frequently asked Linda to put a heating pad on her back. However, one night, Nicole and Linda fell asleep and left the pad on high power for too long on Nicole's back. Because of her paralysis, Nicole had no feeling in her back and couldn't feel the pad burning her skin. As soon as Linda realized what was happening, she removed the pad immediately, but not before Nicole was scarred with a severe burn. When Doug saw the wound, he writhed in sympathy pain. It was one time he was happy Nicole had no feeling in her back.

One of the things that had been sustaining Nicole throughout her illness was the company of her friends. She loved when they stopped by to spend time with her. She loved to listen to the latest gossip from school. She especially loved to hear about their love lives and the boy stories. Unfortunately, lately fewer and fewer friends were stopping by. It upset Nicole and her parents very much. At the time she most needed people, they were seemingly pulling away. When Linda called the school to voice her concern, she learned that there was a rumor going around saying that Nicole was doing poorly and that the family didn't want visitors. Linda let the school administration know that yes it was true, Nicole wasn't doing well, but the idea that they didn't want visitors wasn't the case at all. Afterwards, the school administrators called her classmates together and dissolved the rumor. Then the flow of friends into the house began again.

At a medical evaluation, Nicole reported to the doctors that she was beginning to feel the same tingling sensations in her arms that she used to feel in her legs. After examining and evaluating Nicole, the doctor turned to Linda and said, "Could you step outside, Mrs. Sheriff?" Then he whispered, "We need to talk about DNR."

Nicole overheard him and stopped him in his tracks as he was headed for the door when she said, "You don't have to step out. I know what that means."

He turned to her and asked, "What does it mean?"

"Do not resuscitate. And I'm telling you right now, I don't want anything done to me if it comes to that. I don't want to be a vegetable and be a burden to my parents. When it's time, it's time."

The doctor, who was now speechless, could only look at Linda, who turned her hands palms up and shrugged. "I think she knows what she wants," Linda said.

The doctor then went on to explain to both Linda and Nicole that the paralysis would continue to creep up her body. He recommended that the Sheriffs look into getting more help with the hospice nurse. Pretty soon Nicole was going to need someone with medical experience to look after her.

———

On the day Doug's sister Jody and her husband Gary arrived from their home in Louisiana to be with Nicole, Doug, and Linda for a few days, the sunroom was finally finished. Doug carried Nicole down from her upstairs bedroom. He made her close her eyes, and then he unveiled the room Nicole designed herself. It was just as she had envisioned.

It was twelve feet by twelve feet, with windows on three sides. The side leading to the kitchen had an archway and a serving window in place of where the old window had been. Nicole had decided to decorate using an Italian motif. Two white love seats were arranged under the windows. In the center of the back row of windows was a water fountain. The slanted ceiling was covered with a burgundy and beige striped canvas and a hanging ceiling fan. Three walls were covered with burgundy shingles and one was beige with light green sponge painting. Grape vines hung on each wall and over the fountain. A television was mounted high in one corner. Over the door to the outside, Nicole had a sign hung that read: Live well. Love much. Laugh often. On another wall hung a sign which read: Love is patient, kind, trusting.

Doug gently placed Nicole onto a couch. "This is your new room, Sweet Pea."

"I love it," Nicole said. "It's just the way I want it."

———

Over the next few days, the Sheriffs realized the couches were too uncomfortable for Nicole to stay in for any length of time. What she really needed was a hospital bed, and so Doug talked to the hospice nurse who found a way of procuring one and had it delivered to the house. With the new bed in place, the room became the only place Nicole stayed.

———

As the days passed by, there were a few constants in the Sheriff household. Susan Carlson and Lucy were there almost every day. Nicole and Lucy had developed a bond over time that made them inseparable. Sue would bring her into the house and put her down, and in seconds Lucy would find her way onto Nicole's lap. Nicole still enjoyed talking with Sue and still continued to share some of her deepest and most personal thoughts only with her.

The other constant in the house now was the steady stream of friends that filled Nicole's room. Once the friends had been made aware by the guidance counselors at school that Nicole still cherished their visits, some combination of Nicole's closest friends came to the house each day after school. Sometimes they would get their homework done while watching TV with Nicole.

Other times they would talk about what was new and interesting at school. Often times, they reminisced about the fun times they had when Nicole was younger and healthy. Each day at school, the girls would talk and confirm who was going to Nicole's house right after school and who would go in the evening.

No one except Nicole commented on how physically different she now appeared. The medication she was on made her constantly hungry and she wasn't above eating three or four ice cream sundaes in one day. Because of the eating and the steroids, she was always in need of clothes the next size up.

"Dad, I know I'm getting heavy," she said one day.

"And how do you know that?" Doug asked.

"When I smile, my cheeks touch my glasses." The she added, "I saw myself in the mirror the other day. I didn't even recognize that person. That's not me, I said."

No, that's not you, Doug thought.

Nicole also loved eating Skittles. She actually used this process as therapy. She would concentrate really hard to pick up the small candies and get them into her mouth. Doug silently watched her struggling through this one day. When she finally got a Skittle into her mouth, she looked up at her dad and smiled. The she told him, "My hands are always tingly lately."

"You know what's happening, don't you?" Doug asked.

"I know," Nicole said.

"It's going to be okay though," Doug tried to convince her.

"I know," she lied.

———

The cancer eating its way through Nicole's spine was becoming more painful to endure each day. Finally, the doctors decided to have Nicole go to the hospital so that they could give her an epidural into her spine to relieve the pain. Susan and Lucy accompanied them. Lucy had lately learned to stay perfectly still in Nicole's arms. When the doctor came into the room, Lucy was cuddled up in Nicole's arms in bed with her. The doctor didn't notice Lucy until she popped her apricot head up when he approached with the needle.

He jumped back in surprise. "What the… Is that a dog in your bed? I've never given an epidural with a dog staring at me!"

Sue stepped in now. "You still haven't! Besides, that's not a dog; that's a poodle. That's a step above a dog."

They all laughed and Sue quickly explained Lucy's presence there. The doctor was open to it and continued on with his procedure. Nicole never felt the needle go in as she stayed totally composed with Lucy perfectly still in her arms.

On Thursday, May 30th, Linda called Doug up at school. "Doug, Nicole wants to have her talk with you," Linda told him. Doug knew what that meant. "I'll be right home," he told his wife.

Sue had forewarned Doug and Linda that at some point close to the end, Nicole was going to ask to speak with them so she could say everything she wanted to say and address any issues she wanted to address. This idea had taken form as a response to Sue's therapeutic mantra question: "What do you have control over?" For the last month, Sue and Nicole's conversations had shifted from, "What if I don't survive?" to "This is how I want my death to be." Nicole had accepted the inevitable, but in that acceptance, Sue had instilled in her a desire and ability to take charge over the things that were in her ability to control. Over this time span, Nicole contemplated how she wanted to die, and she entrusted Sue to carry out her wishes. Of course she wanted her mother and father right next to her. She also wanted Sue and Aunt Jody and Uncle Gary to be there. She had to be holding Lucy. Nicole also wanted to be wearing her Kyle Corver 76er's jersey. In the background, she wanted her dolphin song CD to be playing. She even told Sue which specific tracks should be played. Nicole told Sue that after she passed away, she wanted to be cremated.

Sue also encouraged Nicole to make sure she didn't hold back from saying things that needed to be said before she died. Nicole wanted to die with no regrets and no messages undelivered. When Nicole told her mother she needed to have a talk with people, Nicole was controlling what she could control. This action, however, was also an acknowledgement that the end was near.

When Doug came into Nicole's sunroom, he saw his daughter lying in her hospital bed talking to Sue. When Sue saw Doug, she nodded at Nicole and quickly exited the room so Nicole and Doug could be alone. Doug went in and sat on the bed close to Nicole.

"What's up, honey?" he asked.

She started to cry.

"What's wrong?"

"I'm scared, Daddy. I'm scared."

Doug stayed calm and spoke in a soothing tone. "What are you scared of?"

"I'm afraid I'm not going to know anybody in heaven."

"What does God tell us in the Bible? Everyone will know you and you will know everyone. There are no strangers in heaven."

Nicole nodded in agreement. "I know that," she said.

"So then what else is bothering you?"

"I don't want to leave you. I'm going to miss you and I don't want to leave you. I want to see you." It was the first time she had admitted to Doug that she was dying. They had both always been optimistic. But here, as they held each other and rocked back and forth, they both were acknowledging her fate. Nicole sobbed in her father's arms. Her tears merged with Doug's as he put his head next to hers and continued to talk in soothing tones.

"The Bible tells us that to you it will be a blink of an eye before we see each other again. Sweetheart, it will be hard for Mommy and Daddy because for us, the years will seem like a long, long time."

"I don't want to be alone," Nicole confessed.

"You'll never be alone, Sweet Pea. When you let go of our hand, God's hand will be there to take yours, so you'll never be alone."

She contemplated her father's words and then nodded in agreement with them. Her sobs slowed. Then, with the exception of a few uncontrollable heaves, she was done crying. That had always been Nicole's way; let it out in full force so it was over and done with. Then it was time to move on.

Linda came into the room now and the three of them began to discuss the future of the Angel 34 Foundation. "We have to continue to fund the ICEE machines," Nicole insisted.

"Honey, I promise that the foundation will continue. Mommy and I will make sure of it," Doug told her.

"I plan to work for the foundation full time one day," Linda said.

"Mommy, you won't get paid. How are you going to do that?" Nicole asked.

"Don't worry about that," Linda told her. "I'll find a way."

"We have to continue with the scholarships too," Nicole stated. She was referring to the medical scholarships they had set up through the foundation to give to students going into the medical field. "You never know who will have the answer- who will have the cure. You never know what nurse will make a difference in a child's life."

"We'll keep that going too," Doug promised.

"And Daddy, make sure you continue to help the families of kids who have cancer," Nicole persisted. "It's not right that parents should have to worry about paying bills or being at work when their child is sick." That was something that always bothered Nicole. The first night she spent in CHOP, she became aware that not all parents were like her own. She came to know how lucky she was to have a mother who never left her side, who never let her sleep alone from the day she was diagnosed with cancer. She also knew she was fortunate that her parents had such good healthcare plans that they could afford to pay for her care. She heard of parents who lost their homes and their cars trying to pay medical bills for their children. She saw children die without their parents next to them because the parents had to be at work and couldn't be next to their sick children. "It's not right," she declared. "It's just not right! I want the foundation to take care of those children because every child needs an angel."

Nicole was comforted by Doug and Linda's promise that not only would they keep the foundation alive, they would make it grow so it would help thousands of other kids long after Nicole was gone.

A little later that night, Doug peaked in on Nicole, who was sitting up in her bed, lost in her own thoughts. "How you doing?" Doug asked her.

"Good," she replied.

"You're going to have to come up with a better word than good," he told her.

"Excellente!!" she declared.

"Now you're going to try your Spanish on me, huh?" he asked.

They both laughed. Once again, he was awed by her resiliency.

<center>~~~~~</center>

That night, Doug and Linda decided it was time to begin making arrangements for Nicole's funeral. When Sue found out their intentions, she let them know that Nicole had already decided how she wanted to spend her final moments and what she wanted done after her death. Doug and Linda were shocked that Nicole had already thought this through and that she had shared these thoughts with Sue and not them. But Nicole's death had been the one thing the Sheriffs couldn't share with each other openly.

When Sue let Doug know that Nicole wanted to be cremated, he was somewhat relieved. In their conversations with each other, Doug and Linda had also decided that they wanted to have Nicole cremated. The other thing Nicole didn't want was an open viewing. Once again, Doug and Linda had views similar to their daughter's. They didn't want to have an open casket because they didn't want people to remember Nicole by the way she looked now. As far as Doug and Linda were concerned, that girl in the hospital bed wasn't Nicole; not the Nicole they would remember. And *that* Nicole would be celebrated in a memorial ceremony Nicole had planned.

On Friday, when Doug left the house, he told Nicole he had to stay late at school that day and wouldn't be home his normal time. In reality, he had made an appointment with Dave Heintzelman, the local funeral director. He wanted to take his time now and have all arrangements set for whenever Nicole passed. He knew it wouldn't be something he could do when the actual time came.

Doug explained to Dave how they were going to have Nicole cremated. "I know I need to pick out an urn. She loves dolphins. I don't know if you would have anything like that," Doug said.

"You're not going to believe this," Dave said excitedly. "I just received a one of a kind urn made by a guy who designs them. It's decorated with a group of jumping dolphins!"

Doug saw it and knew immediately it was the perfect holder for Nicole's ashes.

~~~

On Saturday, Linda's friend Cheryl came to the Sheriff house with one of her friends who practiced Reiki, a type of holistic healing practice in which a therapist manipulates a person's energy field in an effort to restore the body into a state of balance. The woman who usually performed Reiki on Nicole couldn't make her appointment with Nicole that day because the woman's daughter had gotten into an accident. Linda happened to mention this to her friend Cheryl during the week, and by some unlikely stoke of luck, Cheryl happened to have a friend who practiced Reiki who was available to spend time with Nicole.

The woman spent almost two hours with Nicole, getting a sense of Nicole's body rhythms and inner spirit and attempting to ease her discomfort. When she was finished, she left Nicole alone in the sunroom and walked through the kitchen and into the living room where Doug and Linda were waiting.

"So how did it go?" Doug asked.

"Very good," the woman replied. "Nicole is very relaxed. Physically, her body will not last much longer, but her spirit is not ready to go yet. I asked Nicole why and she said she was waiting for her Aunt Jodie and Uncle Gary to visit again. Are they expected soon?"

"They'll be here tomorrow afternoon," Doug said.

"Good," the woman said, "Because Nicole will probably not see Monday." The woman spoke calmly. She chose her words very carefully. Though they came from her when she spoke them, they seemed to mystically come from some other place. She began to explain what was happening with Nicole's spirit and what would happen in the next day or two to come.

"I told Nicole there are three angels waiting for her," the woman began. "Nicole asked me who they were and became very upset when I couldn't tell her who they were. I just know they are waiting for her." She looked around. Doug and Linda nodded as if they understood what she was referring to. The woman went on. "I told her the birds will tell her when it's time to go?"

"The birds?" Linda asked. "What does that mean?"

"The birds will let you know when it's time. That's all I can say." With that, she walked out of the house and waited outside for Cheryl.

———

The rest of the day Nicole's friends kept vigil by Nicole's side. Word had gotten out that the end was near. All her friends wanted to do was to be close to Nicole. They knelt by her and crawled into the bed with her. Nicole was extremely uncomfortable and sometimes fell asleep. Still, the girls stayed and held Nicole's hands or caressed her face. Nicole appeared to be drifting in and out of sleep. Sometimes it was just easier for her to keep her eyes closed. But it became very clear that whether she had her eyes open or closed, she was cognizant of all that was going on around her. At one point there was a group of six or seven friends with her in the room. Some were in the bed with her. Others were sprawled out on the floor. Nicole's eyes were closed and she appeared to be asleep. Doug looked in on them and wanted to capture the moment. He went and got his camera. "Hey you guys, I want to get a picture of you with Nicole," he called to them. They all moved closer to her. "On the count of three. One. Two. Three." Just at the moment he was about to snap the shot, Nicole opened her eyes wide and smiled. It made for a great photo.

In the evening, her friends took turns saying goodbye to her. They weren't sure if she would still be alive the next day. They kissed Nicole and hugged her and told her that they loved her. Nicole expressed her gratitude for having such great friends and told them that she would miss them. As the friends were leaving, Nicole asked one in particular to stay for a moment longer.

Danielle came back towards Nicole's bed and sat down next to her. She was perplexed as to why Nicole had singled her out. She hadn't been around much the past few months. She was once a vital member of this band of friends. But over the last year she had drifted away. She had spent more time with Nicole today than she had in the previous months combined.

Nicole opened her eyes and looked up at Danielle. "I'm worried about you, Danielle," Nicole started.

Danielle grabbed her hand. "Don't worry about me," she said.

"I am. I've heard the girls talking about you and what you've been doing. I just don't want you to ruin your life."

Danielle knew immediately that Nicole was referring to her experimenting with pot and alcohol. She surmised the other girls must have been talking about her when she wasn't around. She looked down at Nicole and saw Nicole crying over her. She felt the tears streaming down her own face. She was ashamed of some of the things she had done. But she was even more ashamed that her dying friend was upset because of those things.

Nicole went on. "You're too good of a person, Danielle. You don't need that. Don't ruin your life. You have so much ahead of you."

Danielle couldn't talk. She just nodded her head continually in agreement. Then she hugged Nicole and whispered in her ear, "I promise. I won't do it anymore."

When she got up to leave, she was crying uncontrollably. She left the house without saying a word to Doug or Linda. As the door shut behind Danielle, Doug turned to Linda and said, "I'll bet we won't see her tomorrow. She won't be back."

Doug was shocked the next day when Danielle was the first friend to arrive. She had come over earlier than most visitors usually arrived and got to spend some more time alone with Nicole. At one point when Doug looked in on them, they were sound asleep in the bed, holding each other in a comforting embrace.

The rest of that Sunday was similar to the day before. Friends of Nicole came and went all day long. Nicole was especially happy to see her friend Emily, and Emily was relieved to see Nicole. Emily wasn't at the house the day before because she was away on a religious retreat since Friday. She had known Nicole's condition was sliding fast and she concerned she wouldn't get to see Nicole before she passed. All weekend long she was angry with God for letting this illness happen to her friend. She wasn't in the mood to rejoice in his love. She just wanted to get back home so she could see Nicole.

It just so happened that when Emily came over, there were no other friends there and she got to spend some quality time with Nicole. They had been friends the longest, since they were both three, and there was a special bond between them. Emily brought Nicole a chicken potpie her mother had made. Nicole had always loved Emily's mom's chicken potpie. The piecrust broke and they laughed about it.

Emily was always strong and able to stay calm in emotional situations. She prepared herself before hand to stay strong and to not break down in front of Nicole. For two hours, they shared personal thoughts and memories, and then Emily had to go. When she said goodbye, she wouldn't let herself cry. She walked home alone. And as she walked the streets that she and Nicole had walked together a thousand times, she gave in to the feeling of despair that overwhelmed her and allowed herself to cry for her friend that she already missed.

Coach Deb Anthony also stopped by the house. Nicole was happy to see her. She had been such a blessing in her life. They talked about the past field hockey season and Nicole's work as a coach. Then Nicole surprised Coach Anthony when she said, "And you know what? I think I'm going to try playing softball again." Coach Anthony obligingly told her she should do that.

In the late afternoon, Nicole's Uncle Gary and Aunt Jodie arrived. Nicole was so excited to see them. Linda made lasagna, Nicole's favorite food, for dinner. The last guests left the house in the early evening and Nicole settled into her bed for the night.

Around four o'clock in the morning on May 3 2004, Linda woke up Doug. "Doug, Nicole's having trouble breathing," she informed him. "She's really laboring."

Doug came down into Nicole's room and listened for a moment to his daughter struggling just to breathe. "Are you alright, Sweet Pea?" he asked. She nodded yes, but continued to struggle to breathe. He immediately opened up all of the windows in the room. It was still dark outside, but a cool morning breeze found its way into the room. Doug picked up the phone and called Sue Carlson. She had been ever present through Nicole's whole ordeal, and they had agreed she needed to be there in the end. Then he awoke Gary and Jodie. "This may be it," he told them as he awakened them. They were up immediately. The hospice nurse was attending to Nicole, checking all of her vital signs. Linda looked at Nicole and asked her, "Do I need to call the pastor?"

"No. Not yet," Nicole replied.

Nicole was coherent. She was able to talk and let them know what she wanted. All of the sudden she became extremely uncomfortable and restless. Doug and Gary worked together shifting her body in an attempt to find a comfortable position. Each time they would move her and settle her into a new position, she shook her head no and moaned. Around 4:30 they found a comfort spot and Nicole stopped groaning and was able to settle down.

Linda asked Nicole again, "Do I need to call the pastor yet?"

Nicole nodded and said, "Yes, Mommy. Call him. It's time."

Pastor Gary took only fifteen minutes to arrive. He went right to work administering last rites to Nicole. She responded to him throughout the ritual.

Then Nicole asked Linda to put on her dolphin music and

Doug to get her Kyle Korver 76ers jersey. Doug draped the jersey over Nicole and she closed her eyes and listened to the music. It was exactly what she had envisioned. She was surrounded by the people she most loved and they had created the setting she had been envisioning for some time. Doug came closer to hold her, but she whispered to him, "Can you change that song. I don't like that one." He immediately did and was back at her side.

Doug and Linda positioned themselves up close to Nicole's face. Doug held her and Linda stroked her face and hair. "We love you so much," Doug and Linda whispered to her. "I love you too," Nicole responded. "I love you both so much." They repeated their expressions of love for each other several times.

At 4:55 Doug lifted his head off of Nicole's pillow. "Do you hear that?" he asked of everyone in the room. "I hear it," Linda said. They all nodded that they too were hearing it. Outside the window, the darkness had come alive in a riot of sound. There was a cacophony of birds chirping in unison. Their variety of calls was shrill and incessant. The sound built into a crescendo until it dominated the morning air and filled the room.

"Nicole," Linda called. "Nicole. Do hear the birds? Do you hear that sound?"

"I hear them," Nicole said. "I hear them."

"What are they saying?" Linda asked her.

"I don't know yet, but I'll let you know."

Doug was back to holding Nicole and talking closely in her ear. "Remember your trip to Cancun and how you swam with the dolphins. Remember those dolphins, Sweet Pea." He was caressing her face.

Nicole's eyes opened up. "Hey, Ted. Ted's here. How you doing?"

At hearing this, Sue had to leave the room. She was so

overwhelmed that she broke down completely. Ted was her poodle that died several years ago. Sue always had him at school and used him as part of her counseling therapy with her troubled students. He had died of cancer.

"Do you see Ted?" Linda asked Nicole.

"Yes. He's soft and fuzzy and black. And he's here for me."

The adults all looked at each other in amazement. Then Nicole said, "Mommy, it's Grammy. Hi, Grammy." Linda knew Nicole was talking to her mother.

Then Nicole grew very peaceful and still. At 5:00 exactly, Nicole took her last breath. At the same time the birds outside grew silent. For a moment, everything was perfectly still.

In the dawn twilight, Nicole's face glowed. Linda and Doug continued to kiss it.

"Doug, did you see her hands?" his sister Jodie asked. "Did you see what she did?"

He shook his head no. He had been up by Nicole's head and was looking at her face.

Jodie went on. "Right before she took her last breath she raised up her right hand as if to grab hold of something." Gary and the pastor had witnessed this too. Nicole had raised a hand that she hadn't been able to move for the past two weeks because it was paralyzed.

"She raised it right up," Jodie described again.

Doug turned to the pastor. "If I ever doubted in my mind that God or heaven exists, Nicole just removed all of it."

Jodie spoke for all of them when she said, "That was the most beautiful thing I have ever seen."

Epilogue

The Immediate Aftermath

Like he had so many times over the last several weeks, Doug Sheriff carried his daughter. Only this time, when he placed her gently into the vehicle that would take her to the funeral home, he and Linda had to face the harsh reality that she was never coming home again. But the Sheriffs would not grieve alone. The whole town of Northampton grieved right along with them. As word spread in school that morning that Nicole had passed, students and teachers wept openly with each other. They found solace in each other's arms. Nicole's friends were thankful for the time they had spent with her the past weekend.

Nicole's friend Danielle had been awakened that morning at exactly 5:00. Her chest was tight and she was having trouble breathing. And then it passed. Later that day at school she was made aware of the fact that Nicole died at exactly that time.

True to Nicole's wishes, there was no wake, no viewing of a lifeless corpse that had little resemblance to the body it had been for most of Nicole's life. There was a memorial service the following Saturday. It went off exactly as Nicole had planned it with Sue

Carlson. Over a thousand people attended the service. Many more were turned away. Nicole had chosen the songs she wanted sung and the verses she wanted read. Her friends read poems in her honor and some spoke about their memories of Nicole. However the event that tugged on everyone's emotions the most was when Doug spoke about his daughter. He would later say it was Nicole speaking through him, but on this day, Doug delivered a passionate and emotional eulogy that somehow captured the complete essence of Nicole's life and purpose. Somehow he held himself together throughout his delivery. The same couldn't be said for anyone else who was in the church with him that day.

Lucy

Sue Carlson introduced Lucy into Nicole's life the very first day Sue began homebound instruction with Nicole. The rambunctious poodle and the ailing teenager became steadfast friends. In the end, Lucy was constantly in Nicole's arms, comforting Nicole from her ailments and distracting her from her physical torment. After Nicole passed, Doug and Linda insisted that Sue bring her to the memorial service. Throughout all of the eulogies and songs, Lucy kept vigil right on the altar.

The next day, Sue noticed a small bruise on the poodle's skin. Throughout the day it kept getting bigger and bigger. Finally, Sue brought the dog to her veterinarian. After conducting several tests, the vet diagnosed Lucy with a fatal blood disorder. Lucy died the next morning at five o'clock, the exact time Nicole had passed just six days earlier.

Ben

Nicole's friend Ashley reported that Ben told her he regretted breaking up with Nicole so much. But he was scared. He didn't know how to handle the whole situation. Nicole's friend Brittany said that throughout ninth grade, Ben kept a photograph of Nicole in his locker.

The Evolution of the Angel 34 Foundation

When Nicole was an athlete, she was known for her feistiness and determination. She had an indomitable spirit that positively infected her teammates. She exhibited those same traits throughout her battle with Ewing sarcoma. She was determined not to be "just another statistic." She was resolute in her intentions to beat this disease.

Throughout her fight, she never wallowed in self-pity. Instead she chose to make it her mission to help others, to make a difference in this world. In her mind, this battle for her life was no different than any athletic contest. As an athlete, she was going to go down swinging. She would never give up. She was always hoping for the comeback, the miraculous last second shot.

Great players are great teammates. They make the other players around them better. Nicole's self-appointed mission was to make life better for others. She was going to be a great teammate to the other sick children of the world. She had a propensity for helping others and believed that there were so many children who were far worse off than she was. It was this kind of thinking that generated the idea of the Angel 34 Foundation.

The family decided to use Nicole's uniform number in the Foundation's name because of what it stood for. When Nicole and Doug would watch those old films of Walter Payton running for the Chicago Bears, Nicole noticed that she never saw Payton dance or excessively celebrate after he scored a touchdown. Doug explained to Nicole that Payton would always say, "Other people made my success possible. The touchdown is not about me."

Nicole was impressed with this philosophy and came to embody it. On all of her sports teams, she always wore number 34. When she got sick, the number 34 seemed to pop up in all different daily occurrences, so she came to see the number as her angel. She hoped the number could be the angel that could help other sick children.

In developing the Foundation's mission, the family focused on five wishes Nicole had for helping children who were stricken with cancer.

Wish One – ICEES for All Children with Cancer

The foundation grew out of Nicole's efforts and desire to have ICEE machines placed in every children's hospital across the United States and beyond. It was by luck or coincidence that Nicole found out how much those frozen drinks soothed many of her side effects from chemotherapy and radiation. And because Nicole's natural inclination was to help others, she wanted to share her findings on the benefits of ICEES with others. It was Nicole's wish that other children could also be comforted and relieved by these sweet and refreshing treats.

One of the cornerstones of the Foundation is its association with the ICEE Company. As a result of Nicole's initial field hockey fundraiser, the ICEE Company implemented the Angel 34 ICEE Program. Through this program, any children's hospital in the United States that requests an ICEE machine, will receive one free of charge. The Angel 34 Foundation's role in the program is to provide the funding to keep the machines in operation. This includes supplying the syrup for the machines and overseeing their upkeep. In Nicole's lifetime, she was able to know that ICEE machines were in place in three hospitals. As of today, that number has tripled to nine. The Foundation's goal is to oversee the installation of ICEE machines in all 130 children's hospitals across the United States. The Angel 34 ICEE Program is a testament to the fact that Nicole's actions during her lifetime will continue to affect people even though she is no longer living.

The ICEE Company has maintained its commitment to the Angel 34 ICEE Program and even continues to expand its efforts in helping cancer victims. The company has created a new formula for ICEES specifically designed for cancer patients. This formula includes the vitamins and nutrients child cancer patients who are undergoing chemotherapy or radiation need. What Nicole found as a cool comfort, has evolved into something with a real medicinal benefit.

In addition, in 2007, the Angel 34 Foundation purchased a one of a kind ICEE van which is driven to local activities, sporting events and festivals where people are served ICEEs for a donation to the Foundation. Each year, the van travels to more than 40 events.

Wish Two – Help for Families to Finance the Battle

Many doctors believe that a large percentage of deaths from cancer occur not because the disease couldn't be cured or contained, but because people don't have adequate healthcare. Nicole saw first hand that there were people who weren't able to receive certain medications and therapies because they simply couldn't afford them. Nicole was fortunate that both her parents had good healthcare plans. However, there were still many out of pocket expenses the Sheriffs had to handle on their own. They often wondered what people who didn't have decent healthcare coverage did.

At fourteen years old, Nicole had become knowledgeable about the inequities between those who had good insurance and those who didn't. She saw so many children who faced their disease virtually alone because their parents were out working so that they could attempt to keep up with the insurmountable medical bills. "It's not fair," Nicole would often say. "It's not right that families should have to worry about medical expenses when their child is suffering."

One of Nicole's hopes was that the Angel 34 Foundation could provide financial help to such families. The Foundation members ask hospitals to let them know of any families with a cancer-suffering child whose family is struggling financially. The Foundation will pay off bills and purchase such things as wigs and medicines for families. The Foundation does not give a lot of money towards cancer research. This was Nicole's intention. "There are a lot of organizations that raise money for research," Nicole used to say. But she understood that most children who have Ewing sarcoma or any other cancer now won't benefit from that research. "I want to help families now," Nicole said. "I want to help kids who are going through what I am going through." Nicole saw children or heard about children who died without their families around them. She saw children going through therapies with no family support because their parents were out working to pay off medical expenses.

Before she died, Nicole wanted to speak with two people, Oprah Winfrey and Pennsylvania's U.S. Senator Arlen Specter to talk about children's rights. She believed that all children had the right to the best healthcare and that no child should suffer through an illness alone. She thought if she could get these two influential people to address these issues, she could improve the lives of sick children and their families.

She chose Oprah because the popular TV talk show host was known for rallying her viewers to support similar causes. The Sheriffs attempted to contact Oprah several times, but they never received a response. They understood that Oprah was inundated with these types of requests each day. Still, they maintained hope that Nicole would be able to champion her cause on Oprah's show before Nicole grew too ill. Unfortunately, that event never took place.

Nicole had also chosen to contact Senator Specter because she knew he was the chairperson for the House Appropriations Committee. He agreed to meet with her and they set a date. Regrettably, Nicole was unable to keep the appointment. By mid May of her final year she was suffering from shingles so severely that the pain was too much to bear and she had to cancel the meeting. Doug saved the note cards Nicole had made for the meeting. On them, she outlined many of the problems of the healthcare system as it related to terminally ill children. She highlighted what rights she thought all sick children deserved.

After her death, Doug was able to meet with Specter in Nicole's place and he shared Nicole's notes and thoughts with the Senator. Doug and Linda appreciated the Senator's generosity of his time and his promise to see if there was something he could do to advance some of Nicole's ideas. Sadly, not long after this meeting, Senator Specter was diagnosed with cancer himself.

Today, it's obvious the healthcare system is still not fixed and many families are still struggling with the financial burden of medical bills. In an attempt to carry out Nicole's wish, the Foundation continues to try to unburden whatever families it can from the costs associated with cancer.

Wish Three – Fund Scholarships for People Going Into the Medical Field

The third component of the Angel 34 Foundation's purpose is to provide scholarships to men and women who are entering the medical field. Nicole came to understand the many different layers that make up the medical delivery system. She was assisted by people with such diverse backgrounds and specialties, from lab technicians to x-ray technicians, from hospice nurses to emergency room nurses, from stem cell researchers to on-line medical advisors, from Rakai healers to the leading oncology doctors. Nicole realized that every single person in the medical field is important and any one of them may hold a key to defeating cancer.

That is why she wanted to make sure that the Foundation made scholarships available to people choosing to go into the medical profession in any capacity. She didn't want anyone to be denied the opportunity to contribute to the medical profession. As she told her dad, "You never know who is going to find the cure." With this in mind, the Angel 34 Foundation created its medical arts scholarship program. As of this edition, the Foundation has already contributed over $115,000 to people entering the medical field.

As an offshoot to this mission, the Angel 34 Foundation has a scholarship program arrangement with the Big 33 high school all-star game in Pennsylvania. Begun in 2004, the Foundation provides a $500 scholarship in the name of a chosen Pennsylvania player to his high school. That player, in turn, wears a number 34 jersey in honor of Nicole during the game against the Ohio all-star team.

Wish Four – Continue to Support the Pet Therapy Program
Sue Carlson introduced Lucy to Nicole. Throughout Nicole's illness, Lucy was by her side. Her presence had a significant calming power over Nicole. Lucy offered Nicole comfort and friendship. She consoled Nicole and cheered her up. She listened to Nicole's innermost thoughts. Doug and Linda often wonder how much more difficult Nicole's battle would have been had Lucy not been there to endure it with her. For this reason, Nicole insisted that the Foundation should sponsor additional pet therapy

programs. She wanted to make sure other sick children would also have the benefit of a pet companion as they undergo their treatments for cancer.

Today, Sue Carlson is retired from school counseling and is living in Georgia. Here, she is working with a new therapy dog named Lizzy. Sue handpicked Lizzy when she went to see Nancy Murray, a breeder of standard poodles. In the litter of 14 pups, Sue picked out the one that was dashing about and turning all around in circles. When Sue asked the name of the rambunctious pup with the pink collar, she was taken aback when Nancy told her the pup's name was Lizzy. Nicole's middle name was Elizabeth. Sue went on to explain Nicole's story to Nancy. Nancy was so moved by it that she donated the $1500 poodle to the Foundation.

Today, Sue's work and Lizzy's upkeep is financially supported by the Angel 34 Foundation.

In addition, the Foundation received a grant sponsored by Pennsylvania State Senator Lisa Boscola for its Pet Therapy Program. With that money, The Foundation purchased Hope and Simba, two dogs that visit local hospitals and bring comfort and support to sick children.

Wish Five - Support the St. Jude Children's Hospital

Doug remembers watching the St. Jude telethons with Nicole. They sent in small donations to help the fight against cancer. In desperation, Nicole called St. Jude's out of desperation when the tide in her battle with Ewing sarcoma was turning against her. The doctors there were supportive and kind. They offered support for Nicole and consulted with Nicole's attending physicians regarding how to treat patients in the more advanced stages of the disease.

Nicole decided that St. Jude Children's Hospital in Knoxville, Tennessee would be the one research facility that the Angel 34

Foundation would support. Each year, the Foundation would make a yearly donation to support this facility. In 2005, the Foundation donated over $4000 to St. Jude Children's Hospital. The members of the Foundation hope to be able to continually increase the amount of this annual donation.

Deb Anthony's Own Battle

Coach Deb Anthony was an angel to Nicole when Nicole needed one. Coach Anthony found a place for Nicole in her field hockey program. She gave Nicole an important role on the team and tutored Nicole in the art of coaching. In an era when so many people are worried about being sued for their actions, Coach Anthony allowed Nicole to play despite the fact that she didn't have medical clearance to do so. The Sheriffs and she were completely aware that the board of education policy was not being followed. Neither the Sheriffs nor Coach Anthony cared. If Nicole got hurt in the game she entered, Coach Anthony knew she had no fear of the Sheriffs suing the school for neglect. They all acted in the best interest of a child who was dieing from cancer.

Ironically, in the fall of 2005, Coach Anthony was diagnosed with breast cancer. Supporting Coach Anthony the way she supported Nicole, Doug and Linda were with the coach when she broke the news to her team.

Fortunately, the cancer was detected early and treated quickly. Today, Coach Anthony is retired from coaching and teaching at Northampton High School.

Doug and Linda Today

Doug and Linda promised their daughter that they would keep the foundation alive and that they would never stop helping people who suffered from cancer. In 2006, after 20 years in public education,

Doug, at the age of 44, retired from his job as the Athletic Director of Saucon Valley High School. This move allowed Doug to begin working full time on the Angel 34 Foundation. Today, Doug spends most of his time planning and running fund raising events as well as overseeing the finances and public relations of the Foundation. He visits local hospitals and schools and gives motivational speeches in an effort to inspire people to be champions in their communities. Linda is still working at PPL but spends much of her free time doing Foundation work. She hopes to retire soon so that she could join Doug in working on the Foundation full-time,

In March of 2007, Doug and Linda purchased property and a home on 3.6 acres in Nazareth, Pennsylvania. They spent more than a year renovating the home and turning it into what is now called Angel Field. This facility, for which Doug and Linda are the caretakers, functions as a retreat for children who are battling cancer and their families.

The incidents involving number 34 continue to take place. Doug swears it is Nicole's way of letting him know Nicole is still close at hand. Doug has been cut off on the highway by a car with a license plate number of 3434. The bill for a meal at which Foundation ideas were discussed in detail came to $34.34. And most significantly, at the Northampton girls basketball game that was held in remembrance of Nicole, the score at the end of regulation was 34-34.

On Nicole's 18th birthday, the Angel Field home and all of its belongings were donated to the Angel 34 Foundation. The Foundation has been incorporated and has a board of trustees who assist in determining its direction. However, that direction never wavers far from the five-wish plan Nicole created.

For more information regarding the Angel 34 Foundation and its activities and programs, please visit www.angel34.org.